The MAPMAKER
and the GHOST

The MAPMAKER
and the GHOST

SARVENAZ TASH

WALKER BOOKS FOR YOUNG READERS
AN IMPRINT OF BLOOMSBURY
NEW YORK   LONDON   NEW DELHI   SYDNEY

*To Golnaz and Arash for making growing up an adventure.
And to Homa for being my compass.*

First published in the United States of America in April 2012
by Walker Books for Young Readers, an imprint of Bloomsbury Publishing, Inc.
Paperback edition published in March 2013
www.bloomsbury.com

For information about permission to reproduce selections from this book, write to
Permissions, Walker BFYR, 175 Fifth Avenue, New York, New York 10010
Bloomsbury books may be purchased for business or promotional use. For information on bulk
purchases please contact Macmillan Corporate and Premium Sales Department at
specialmarkets@macmillan.com

The Library of Congress has cataloged the hardcover edition as follows:
Tash, Sarvenaz.
The mapmaker and the ghost / Sarvenaz Tash.
p.   cm.
Summary: The summer before starting middle school, when eleven-year-old Goldenrod
Moram sets out to make a very accurate map of the forest behind her home, she discovers
a band of troublemakers, a mysterious old lady, and the ghost of her explorer idol.
ISBN 978-0-8027-2340-6 (hardcover)
[1. Cartography—Fiction. 2. Maps—Fiction. 3. Forests and forestry—Fiction.
4. Ghosts—Fiction 5. Gangs—Fiction. 6. Community life—Fiction.] I. Title.
PZ7.T2111324Map 2012   [Fic]—dc22   2011010978

ISBN 978-0-8027-3439-6 (paperback)

Book design by Nicole Gastonguay
Typeset by Westchester Book Composition
Printed in the U.S.A. by Thomson-Shore, Dexter, Michigan
2 4 6 8 10 9 7 5 3 1

All papers used by Bloomsbury Publishing, Inc., are natural, recyclable products
made from wood grown in well-managed forests. The manufacturing processes
conform to the environmental regulations of the country of origin.

The MAPMAKER
and the GHOST

NO FUN

Goldenrod Moram had a first name that sounded like it belonged in the middle of a fairy tale, where she would be the dazzling princess in need of rescuing. But this couldn't be further from the truth. For one thing, fairy-tale princesses probably didn't get in trouble practically every day of the fifth grade. (Then again, they probably didn't talk back much either.) For another, fairy-tale princesses probably had more than one friend in the whole entire world. (And if they didn't, they at least had servants or courtiers or some such other fan base that could pass for friends.)

But Goldenrod had only been named Goldenrod because her mother was an avid gardener and her father had lost the coin toss on the day of her birth. Had her father won, she might have been named after one of *his* hobbies, which included cooking and amateur house repair. When daydreaming, Goldenrod often thought about all the other things she could have been called and how they all would have been preferable: Oregano Moram, Staple Gun Moram, Brisket Moram, Spark Plug . . .

"Goldenrod!"

Nope, she couldn't escape her name. And here it was being hissed at her by a tall woman with dark hair and pursed lips.

"Yes?"

"Are you going to answer the question or not?" Ms. Barbroff pointed at the blackboard with a stiff finger, the purple bags under her eyes moving in time with her words. She was just the sort of teacher who insisted on teaching right up to the last bell of the last day of school.

Goldenrod didn't know the answer, and it seemed like Ms. Barf wasn't about to let her off the hook, even though elementary school was almost over—for good—and even though her very best friend had just moved away to a whole other state and left her to deal with the upcoming ordeal of middle school all alone.

"Goldenrod, have you stopped and considered that this is information you'll actually *need* next year?"

"Not really." Under normal circumstances, she would have relished this opportunity to say something funny. But her heart wasn't in it, not without Charla to come visit her at the principal's office when she inevitably got sent there.

"Well, I suggest you start thinking about it. Sixth-grade math is no joke."

For a second, it looked as if Ms. Barf was going to turn away without further comment. Goldenrod should have known better. "I'm not going to have much more of an opportunity to say this to you, Ms. Moram, but mark my words. If you don't shape up and start paying attention, you're going to spend most of your middle-school career in the principal's office. And that'll lead you straight into the life of a hoodlum. And *then* what will your mother think?"

Goldenrod thought, *She will say, "Oh, if only my daughter had answered that question on negative numbers in the fifth grade. What a world, what a world!"* But Goldenrod didn't say a word, concentrating instead on doodling a rather striking portrait of the Wicked Witch of the West in her notebook. Ms. Barf turned away with a *humph* and continued on with the lesson.

The only highlight of the day was that it ended with Ms. Barf going over Goldenrod's favorite lesson: the five parts of a map. Even though she knew them by heart, and had for at least two years, she perked up as Ms. Barf's booming voice talked about the legend, the scale, the compass rose, the title, and the grid. Just the mere mention of these things made her smile dreamily at the memory of how she and Charla had spent their previous map-filled summer.

All too soon, the lesson was over, and Goldenrod was only one bus ride away from a long, vast stretch of summer vacation. True that she didn't know whom she was going to spend this summer vacation with, but at least she knew it wouldn't be Ms. Barf.

And it wouldn't be Charlie Cookman either, she thought angrily, as she saw the large, muscular oaf in the hallway tormenting some smaller kid eclipsed by Charlie's enormous behind and his equally enormous backpack. Charlie was well known for carrying at least two to three large bottles of energy soda with him in that backpack at all times. His father was an amateur wrestler, and it was rumored that Charlie himself had been lifting dumbbells since the age of six and drinking protein shakes since he could hold a bottle.

"Listen." Charlie's whiny voice drifted over to Goldenrod as she walked past him to catch her school bus. "You're telling me these are all the video games you have on you? Do you expect me to believe that?"

Sometimes it's no fun being a kid, Goldenrod thought, just as she caught a glimpse of a purple backpack and dark brown moppy hair. She felt a bolt in her chest. The smaller, trembling kid Charlie was threatening just happened to be her little brother, Birch. Sometimes it was no fun being a big sister either.

Especially when she'd never been all that big. The only thing both Goldenrod and Birch had inherited from their mother—besides their garden-themed names (their dad was notoriously unlucky at coin tosses)—was her tiny frame, and it looked like this detail was going to make getting out of school on this day extra difficult. *Difficult*, Goldenrod thought, *but not impossible. At least I can put some of my deception training to good use.*

She stood up to her full height of four feet three and a half inches, hoisted her backpack higher, took a deep breath, and marched over to Charlie, her dark brown ponytail swinging with determination.

"Hey," she said once she was right beside him.

Charlie looked confused, as if it was taking his brain some time to understand the one word she had spoken. His mouth gaped open a little, showing his soda-stained teeth and tongue.

Goldenrod took this opportunity to address her brother. "Hey, little bro. Got yourself in trouble, huh?" She smirked. "Serves you right, twerp."

Birch looked mortified, like he couldn't believe his own sister was turning on him at this very humiliating, likely to be physically painful, moment. Even the freckles on his face seemed to redden.

"This is your brother then, huh, Mold-and-rot?" Charlie asked.

Goldenrod knew Charlie must have heard that lovely nickname from one of the other kids—he was definitely too stupid to have come up with it himself.

"Yeah. Take him for whatever he's got. He deserves it.

See you, dunderhead," she said to Birch and turned around to leave.

"Hey, wait a minute," Charlie said, finally starting to catch on. "You mean you actually *want* me to mess with your little brother?"

Goldenrod shrugged. "He's a brat. Always getting me in trouble at home."

"Hey, Charlie." Goldenrod turned to see Jonas Levins, Charlie's trusty sidekick and—most obviously—the brains of their operation. "Hey, man. If Mold-and-rot wants you to mess with him, you better leave him alone."

"How come?" Charlie asked.

"Because," Jonas said a little impatiently, "why would you want to do anything that would make that weirdo happy?"

"Oh. Yeah."

Jonas took Birch's limp hand in his own and shook it. "Keep up the good work, kid. It must be hard, having *that* loser for a sister." He started to laugh and Charlie joined in with his big, wheezy chuckles.

Goldenrod almost walked away. Really, she did. Later on she would tell the school principal this. And her parents. She wouldn't bother telling Ms. Barf, though, because let's face it, it wouldn't have made a bit of difference.

But just then the sight of those two horrid kids standing there, filling her little brother's head with nonsense about her—stuff he didn't ever have to know, really—got the best of her. Yes, she had expected that pretending she wanted them to bully Birch would make the kids leave him alone. But now they had taken it too far. She knew the kids thought she was a weirdo; the last time Jonas had thought she was cool was probably in kindergarten, when they actually still played together at her house. Up until a few months ago, though, at least she was a weirdo with a friend and it didn't matter so much what anyone else thought. Now that she was on her own—well, she just couldn't have her little brother turning on her too.

With one hand, Goldenrod grabbed a sharpened pencil from her case; with the other, she grabbed onto Charlie's backpack and started to shake it, hard.

"What are you doing, you dork?" Charlie shrieked as he tried to pull away.

But before he had the chance to, Goldenrod had stabbed the pencil right into the heart of his backpack. There was a great, loud pop, and suddenly a fountain of orange energy soda shot out of the top of Charlie's half-open backpack and showered down all over his head. Goldenrod, Birch, and Jonas got out of the way just in time. Kids in the hallway started to roar with laughter.

Goldenrod smiled. But the smile wouldn't last long.

"Goldenrod Moram!" a deep voice boomed.

Of course Ms. Barf had to have seen the whole thing. She was pointing a shaking finger at Goldenrod.

"Five minutes! Five minutes before the end of your

career here at Pilmilton Elementary, and *this* is how you choose to send yourself off. I don't know why I should be surprised. To the principal's office, you no-good hoodlum!"

Jonas was the one laughing now, though Charlie still looked too shaken up by his sticky encounter to fully appreciate what was going on.

Birch stared awestruck at Goldenrod. "What about Mom . . . ?"

"Yeah, she's probably going to have to come pick me up now. You can tell her," Goldenrod said softly as she followed Ms. Barf down to the hallway she knew so well.

THE MAPMAKER

As the first Monday morning without school dawned for hundreds of kids all over the town of Pilmilton, Goldenrod was stuck in her room. She was starting her summer vacation grounded for a whole week.

She didn't think that her punishment would have been quite so harsh if Ms. Barf hadn't personally called up her parents and used the words "hoodlum" and "lack of parental discipline" so many times. She had also made a point of calling Goldenrod's crimes "damage to personal property" and "attack with a sharp weapon" and then saying that she wouldn't be surprised if "the victim's" parents took legal action. The thought of Charlie Cookman and his muscles being a victim of anything other than a math test almost made Goldenrod laugh.

Almost, because although she could handle the other

kids being mean to her and she was even used to Ms. Barf's anger, what she really hated was hearing her parents say they were disappointed in her. Which is exactly what they did say before grounding her for a whole week.

So, as the sun shone brightly outside, Goldenrod spent that Monday lying belly-down on her bed, poring over her books—almost all of which were atlases—and thinking about Charla.

Goldenrod and Charla had always loved maps. They found an indescribable thrill in seeing all the possibilities of places to go laid out in front of them on a page, like they could be reached at any time. They loved maps that showed mountain ranges and valleys, and those that showed names of capitals and cities. They even loved the ones that told you which state produced the most sugar snap peas.

One day the previous year, while they were browsing the library for a book of maps they maybe hadn't come across before, Charla found a biography that was haphazardly shelved in that section. It was for two explorers named Meriwether Lewis and William Clark, who, a long time ago, went on a three-year adventure across most of the western United States, making maps and discovering loads and loads of plants and animals that no one had ever known existed, and even getting accidentally shot in the leg while being mistaken for an elk by a nearsighted fellow explorer (well, one of them did anyway—Lewis). Before Lewis and Clark, no one knew that there was land past the Rocky Mountains (which seemed preposterous to Goldenrod and Charla, who actually lived on some of that very land).

From that day forward, Goldenrod and Charla made great plans to be the next Lewis and Clark: explorers, adventurers, and mapmakers. Goldenrod particularly felt a kindred spirit in Meriwether Lewis, in part because he had had to deal with a name as equally ridiculous as her own; Charla was happy to take on the Clark role. Since Lewis and Clark called their crew the Corps of Discovery, Charla and Goldenrod had picked a name for themselves that they thought sounded just as mighty: the Legendary Adventurers. They decided that, along the way, they might have to add some more crew members, perhaps a Sacagawea type, who was the intelligent Native American woman who had been the Discovery Corps's guide and translator. For just then, though, they felt the Legendary Adventurers could flourish in the very capable hands of its two leaders.

The girls spent months training for their adventures. In case they ever needed to hide from a hostile animal, they practiced camouflage techniques, using everything from makeup to mud to stealth moves to blend in with their surroundings. In case they were ever captured by enemies, they practiced interrogation and deception techniques, learning the most effective ways to mislead their captors under pressure by acting out different scenarios and taking turns playing the roles of Legendary Adventurer vs. Formidable Foe. And, of course, they continually honed their map-drawing skills by getting their parents to enlist them in art classes at the Y.

There was only one real glitch in their grand plans: neither Goldenrod nor Charla could think of a single area in the mile-wide radius around Goldenrod's house that called for discovery because, unfortunately, that was exactly as far as Goldenrod was allowed to go without adult supervision. This was definitely one of the drawbacks to being eleven (ten, at the time).

They had had one possible breakthrough: the previous August, Charla's mom had mentioned offhand that they might go camping in the fall and had told Goldenrod that she would be welcome to come if they did. Both Goldenrod and Charla agreed that this was excellent news. Camping meant a forest and trees—in other words, undeveloped land—and that was exactly the type of land that needed exploration.

They eagerly waited for Charla's mom to mention the camping trip again, and in the meantime started collecting some of the supplies they thought they might need. Goldenrod asked for a compass for her eleventh birthday, and Charla asked for *The Encyclopedia of North American Flora and Fauna* for hers.

But in late November, instead of mentioning what was to be the great important camping trip that would change the American landscape forever, Charla's mom announced that her job was moving the family to another state. By February, they were gone.

And now Goldenrod was left alone to look sadly at her books of maps and her beautiful, unused compass sitting in its case on her desk. She sighed and stared out of her second-story window, where she could see her mother in her straw hat and gardening gloves. Mrs. Moram was a very small woman with short, blond hair and tan olive skin that made a perfect contrast to all the bright flowers she was working against. She was joyously bent over her garden now, probably excited that her beloved dahlias and, eventually, goldenrods would soon be in full bloom. *My name could have been Dahlia*, Goldenrod thought to herself. *So much better . . .*

BANG! CLACK! WHACK! She was shaken from her grumpy thoughts by the rooftop sounds of her father, a scientist who had taken a week off to pursue one of his favorite pastimes: fixing rain gutters.

And from downstairs came the beeps and wails of Birch's video game.

It seemed like everyone in the world was having a great time . . . except Goldenrod.

But then again, wallowing is not a good trait for a Legendary Adventurer to have, she thought. In fact, she was almost certain that Meriwether Lewis would never have wallowed had he ever been eleven years old and grounded.

Goldenrod took out a pencil and a fresh sheet of grid paper and, looking out the window again, started to sketch a map of her mother's garden. Chrysanthemums next to the rosebushes next to the magnolia tree. A ring of

soon-to-be-blooming goldenrods surrounding it all—a ring
that her mother had to take very special care of because her
daughter's namesake flowers were the kind that would absolutely run rampant and take over the whole garden if they
weren't carefully monitored.

Suddenly, as Goldenrod squinted out at the flowers,
one of those brilliant a-ha ideas hit her as sharply as the
sun's rays. What if her project for the summer was to make
a map of Pilmilton? Not just any map, though. The most
accurate map in the world. Every house, every tree, every
shrub. Okay, so maybe it wouldn't be as grand or as long an
expedition as the one Lewis and Clark went on, and maybe
she would discover nothing new at all. But then again . . .
maybe she would. And then she could take the best map
and sketches of any new specimens she discovered and mail
them to Charla. That way, she could still be like her long-
distance Clark. Yes!

For the first time in days, Goldenrod felt filled with a
sense of purpose.

✳

On Tuesday, Goldenrod got her backpack ready. She packed:

- a flashlight with extra batteries (those always seemed
  to come in handy in books or movies when anyone
  was going on an adventure)
- three fresh notebooks, one lined for notetaking,

one unlined for sketches, and a third filled with grid paper for the map
- three sharpened pencils
- a pencil sharpener
- her pocket-sized atlas
- a ruler
- a measuring tape
- a clean and empty jelly jar (in case she ever needed to collect any specimens)
- a pair of tweezers (for the exact same reason)
- an old, rather dull pair of her mother's gardening shears
- a set of green and brown face paints that she had saved from last Halloween
- a lunch box for which she was planning many different kinds of sandwiches
- her compass, of course
- a roll of duct tape (she had yet to find any use for this tape herself, but she had heard her father go on and on about its indispensability)
- and a very small, very dirty sock that probably used to be yellow. This was a sock she had worn as a baby and which, for some reason, she found comforting to carry around.

Wednesday and Thursday were spent thinking about how to get her mother to let her step foot outside of the four barriers that she had never been allowed to leave by herself before. The perfect mile-long and mile-wide square was marked on each end by the park playground, Pilmilton Woods, Joseph McKinney's house, and the Pilmilton Science Museum on the corner of Sutton and Main. Knowing her mother, getting permission to explore outside of that area wasn't going to be easy.

By Friday, Goldenrod was standing outside and watching her father happily bang away on the roof. She was making sure that he didn't fall. This was called spotting and it was pretty boring, but Goldenrod had volunteered to do it because she figured that having Dad on her side when she talked to Mom would be crucial in her Barrier-Breaking Plan.

So there she stood in the front yard, her cheap daisy kiddie sunglasses (the only pair she could find) squishing against her temples and hurting her head without providing much protection from the glaring sun.

"You're doing a great job, kiddo," her dad called down with a huge grin. He was a slightly pudgy, dark-haired man and, at the moment, he was sweating profusely. "I feel safer already. Remember, two Morams are better than one."

"Yup," Goldenrod said as she imagined her perfect, detailed map embossed with a Legendary Adventurers logo (which, she realized, she would have to design). "You hungry, Dad?" she called up to him.

"What's the special today?" he called back down, his

face even more freckled than usual because of all the days working in the sun.

"Peanut butter on whole wheat toast with strawberries and Cheerios. For extra crunch." Goldenrod was an excellent sandwich-maker.

"Mmmm. I'll have one of those."

Goldenrod nodded. "Birch!" she called to her little brother.

"What?" he called back from inside.

"Come take my place watching Dad for a sec."

"I'm about to beat Level Three!" he yelled back.

"I'm making sandwiches," Goldenrod said.

She heard a beep and a few seconds later Birch was outside. "For me too?"

"Of course," Goldenrod said and then turned around to the direction of her mom, who was working in the farthest reaches of the front garden. "You want one, Mom?"

There was no response. Her mother was digging.

Goldenrod had to walk over to her and tap her on the shoulder before her mother heard a word she was saying.

In the kitchen, as Goldenrod prepared the four sandwiches, she thought about her backpack. She thought about her map. She thought about leaving the Barriers. She thought about a new school without Ms. Barf. And, most of all, she thought about Charla. It wasn't going to be quite the same, being Lewis without Clark. But still, she knew her friend would be thrilled for her if Goldenrod really were able to become a Legendary Adventurer, make an extraordinary map, and hopefully find something no one even knew existed.

Goldenrod smiled as she plated the sandwiches. When she was done, she rummaged through the kitchen drawers and found a box of frilly toothpicks. She put one on each of the two slices of her mother's sandwich before putting all the plates on a tray and heading back outside. Sometimes, the littlest things could put parents in a good mood. And she needed her mom to be in the best mood possible.

THE EXPLORATION BEGINS

It had taken a few days for Goldenrod to convince her mother to let her go through her impenetrable barriers. Eventually, she had had to pull the Charla card—telling her mother that the only way she could possibly make any new friends would be to leave the house and explore some new places. "Besides, it'll be good for my sense of independence, Mom."

"It's true, Janine," Mr. Moram had chirped from the roof. "Our girl's got to learn to be self-sufficient sometime. Let's face it, she's a middle schooler now. She's not going to find much adventure hanging around the backyard." Goldenrod had smiled innocently, all the while giving herself a mental high five for planting those lines so perfectly in her dad's head.

On the Tuesday after her long, drawn-out grounding,

she found herself at the end of her driveway, looking around with an exhilarating sense of freedom. Her green Backpack of Adventure, which now, needless to say, also contained a cell phone programmed to call her house and 911 with the touch of a button, hung heavy on her back with the promise of great things.

In between scheming about how to get on her mother's best side, Goldenrod had spent a great deal of time mapping out her mapping intentions. She had decided that she would start, like Lewis and Clark, in the west (past the science museum), then east (past Joseph McKinney's house), south (past the park playground), and, finally, north to Pilmilton Woods.

She had carefully filled the first page in her gridded notebook with the five essential parts of the map. She had come up with a legend—a set of symbols—which included representations of trees, bushes, fences, dogs, litter, no-parking signs, sprinklers, wading pools, and pretty much anything else you would expect to see in your standard suburban town. There was a compass rose that pointed out north, south, east, and west. There was a scale to indicate distance. There was a title on top (Town of Pilmilton) and, of course, there were the grid lines themselves. Everything was ready. All that was missing was the map.

That first day, Goldenrod walked straight to the strip mall that housed the science museum, the nail salon, the vitamin shop, and the doctor's office. She strode right up to the very edge of the museum's large gray building and squinted at a bench that was only a few feet away. Yesterday, she would not have been allowed to sit on this bench. But today . . . ah, today, Goldenrod looked out at the scene in front of her and with a finger erased the imaginary fiery red line that her mother had once made for her right past that museum. Then, with a thrill that she could feel even in her elbows, she hopped right over that line and sat down on the bench.

She allowed herself one moment to take it all in. It was another beautiful day, and the sun gleamed off the few cars that were in the strip mall's small parking lot. Tied to a fire hydrant a few feet away was a small, gray, yapping dog. A boy in black leaned against the front of the doctor's office, and an old security guard squinted out at him from the front of the museum.

She had to admit, she felt just a little bit more grown up sitting on this bench all by herself. With a smile, Goldenrod started to rummage around in her backpack. She had work to do.

She took out her graph paper, a sharpened pencil, and her measuring tape. She decided that the park bench was as good a place as any to start, so she drew the tiny symbol she had come up with for it. Then she set about measuring the bench itself. She was able to hook one end of the measuring tape underneath the seat and pull the tape out to the other end. But unfortunately, measuring from the bench to the tree all by herself proved to be much more difficult. Whereas Lewis had Clark, however, Goldenrod at least had duct tape. Mentally making a note to thank her father, she secured one end of the measuring tape and managed to jot down the accurate length that she needed.

As she worked, she suddenly got the feeling that she was being watched. When she glanced up to confirm her suspicions, she took a closer look at the boy in black. She was surprised she hadn't recognized him earlier. The boy wasn't leaning against the front of the doctor's office so much as he was curving into it, and there was only one person—probably in the entire world—who could stand that way.

His name was Drew Henderson. He was two years older than Goldenrod, and he must have spent the thirteen years of his existence perfecting the worst posture imaginable. In fact, he slouched so much that his back formed an almost perfect C when he was standing in his neutral position. Goldenrod had often wished her mother could have gotten a look at Drew every time she told Goldenrod to "stand up straight."

What was truly remarkable about Drew, however, was that he seemed to be able to control his claylike spine in a way most human beings certainly could not. His victory in the elementary school limbo competition a couple of years back was the stuff of legend.

Almost as if the universe was in tune with her thoughts, at that very moment a middle-aged man in a white coat came out of the doctor's office. He stared wide-eyed at Drew and slowly started to circle him. Drew stopped watching Goldenrod and looked lazily at the doctor instead.

"Young man!" the doctor said briskly. "How are you doing that?"

"Doing what?" Drew asked in a slow drawl.

"Standing that way."

Drew smirked and shrugged; only when he did so, he caused his whole spine to go up and down one vertebra at a time, almost like piano keys.

The doctor seemed beside himself with fascination. "You must understand, I'm a doctor, a chiropractor. I've spent years studying the human spine, and I have never, ever seen it manipulated in that way."

"Yeah, I know."

"Tell me, my boy. Have you ever been studied?"

"Studied?"

"Yes," the doctor said. "I feel like I could create a whole paper on you. Would you let me examine you?"

"What's in it for me?"

"Well . . . you'd be doing it in the name of science. Of progress. Of great possible medical breakthroughs."

Drew hesitated for a moment. "Medical breakthroughs?"

"Colossal ones," the doctor said.

"Nah," Drew said. "Not interested."

"I'll give you fifty bucks." The doctor obviously had to have some brains to be a doctor, after all.

"Make it two hundred," Drew said.

"Two hundred?!" the doctor said in alarm.

"All in the name of colossal medical breakthroughs," Drew said.

The doctor thought for a second. "Okay, fine."

"But I can't do it now."

"How about tomorrow? Would you make an appointment with my secretary for then?"

"Maybe. If I get a deposit today."

"A deposit?"

"Fifty bucks. Just so I know you won't bail on me and my valuable time, Doctor."

The doctor was looking grouchy now. "Oh, fine, come along then," he said and led Drew into his office.

Goldenrod was a little angry at herself for getting distracted by the odd conversation, so she immediately got back to work. A few minutes later, she had just finished putting the duct tape down by the edge of the museum door when a large foot almost stepped on her pinkie. She looked up to see Charlie Cookman, carrying two bottles of his orange energy soda and a small striped ball. He did a double take upon seeing her.

"Hey! What are *you* doing here?" he asked her. He said

the word "you" like it was a moldy piece of toast he needed to get out of his mouth as quickly as possible.

She really was about to ask him the same thing. Surely he hadn't just come out of the science museum, as it was highly unlikely that Charlie would be found anywhere near something educational in his spare time. But then Goldenrod glimpsed the small vitamin shop next to the museum and things became a little clearer.

"I'm allowed to be here, you know," she said coolly. "It's a free strip mall." She made a point of glaring at his soda bottles as she gripped her pencil tighter.

Charlie looked a little alarmed and held his soda closer to his body as he walked away. Despite the summer heat, he was wearing a black hoodie, and as he pressed the bottles to it, it was obvious the pockets bulged with something. Goldenrod frowned. *Just what is he up to now?*

Across the street, Drew was coming out of the doctor's office. Charlie went over to him.

"Everything okay?" Drew asked.

"Yeah," Charlie said. "What were you doing in there?"

"Just a little extra business. Come on, let's go," Drew said as they both walked away together, Charlie bouncing his rubber ball.

Distracted again, Goldenrod thought to herself. She really needed to focus a little better if she ever wanted to get her map done.

Ten minutes later, she had an even bigger problem on her hands. Although she had a symbol for dogs on her legend, it was impossible to measure the tiny, yapping dog's exact distance from the hydrant because he kept moving. It made her realize that perhaps it would be necessary to edit down her legend to include only those things that would remain stationary. After all, what good would an extraordinary map be if it was made inaccurate almost the moment she had drawn it?

There was a slight possibility that the dog might be an undiscovered breed, though. True, Goldenrod was pretty sure that the dog was Ulysses, the beloved Labradoodle of Old Sue, who owned the nail salon. *But it never hurts to check*, she thought to herself as she kneeled down and gently picked up one of the dog's tiny paws.

This did not help with the yapping situation, and it wasn't very long before Old Sue herself came walking out of the chiropractor's office.

"What *are* you doing?" She looked at Goldenrod oddly as she untied Ulysses's leash from the hydrant that Goldenrod had hastily started to measure.

"Oh, nothing. Just . . . a little project, Mrs. McNamara." Goldenrod smiled at Old Sue.

Sue continued to look at her a little doubtfully but left with Ulysses without further comment.

The truth was that Goldenrod hadn't told anyone about

her map; she didn't think anybody besides Charla would understand. She'd talked to her parents about wanting to explore Pilmilton but hadn't given the exact reason why. And as Old Sue walked away, eyebrows still arched, Goldenrod thought that she was probably right to keep it to herself.

By five thirty, Goldenrod was exhausted. Not only had she spent the day bending over and duct taping every which way, but she also felt like she had spent it under suspicious scrutiny from everyone from the museum security guard to the chiropractor's secretary to any passersby.

As Goldenrod zipped up her backpack and headed home (she had a strict curfew of six o'clock), she wondered to herself if maybe west was not the way to go first. What Goldenrod needed was somewhere a little more private to start out with, somewhere she could hone her mapmaking speed and precision.

By the time she turned the corner onto her block, she had made her decision. Tomorrow, she would go to the forest. Not only was it the most private part of town, but it was also probably the place most likely to discover uncharted territory or a new variety of flower or furry creature. In other words, the likelihood of it being the most important part of her map was very great, and she could see no reason at all to wait to explore it.

THE OLD LADY WHO LIVES BY THE WOODS

The very next day found Goldenrod standing at the edge of Pilmilton Woods with her backpack and a head full of possibility. She hadn't walked more than thirty steps inside her forest barrier when she saw something that proved her hunch from the day before had been correct. There was a house right on the very edge of the woods that she had never, ever seen before. Had never even known existed! Of course, that wasn't terribly shocking, considering the house was blocked by a grove of very dense maple trees that she had never been allowed to walk behind before. Needless to say, a discovery of this magnitude could prove to be a very important moment in the life of a mapmaker.

The house was small, but looked well kept and cozy. There was a very bright rose garden in the front. Only by walking closer to it did Goldenrod notice the very small old woman who was on her knees, tending to the roses.

The old woman looked up at the sound of approaching footsteps. "Well, hello," she said.

For a moment, Goldenrod was a little startled by how ugly the old woman was. *If this were a fairy tale*, she thought, *this woman might be a witch or a sorceress*. But here, in real life, she was merely exceedingly ugly. She had extremely thin hair that was so white it was almost perfectly clear, showing the freckled and dry scalp underneath. Her nose was very large and accented with an enormous bump that grew out of the middle of it, like a volcano. By contrast, her eyes were very small and close together, so small that it was hard to tell what color they were at all. She had a pair of white bushy eyebrows. Her ears were rather large and protruding. Her teeth were very crooked.

It took Goldenrod a second to realize that she was gawking rudely. "Hello," she finally said, a little embarrassed.

"Are you lost?" the old lady asked.

Goldenrod shook her head. "No. Not at all."

"That's good. It's important to know where you are."

Goldenrod nodded. She was so excited, she didn't quite know where to start. Should she ask the old lady why her house wasn't on a street? Should she just sit and draw everything as quickly as she could?

Before she had enough time to come to a decision, the old lady's sharp eyes had noticed the sketchbook that was tucked beneath Goldenrod's arm.

"Are you planning on drawing something?" she asked.

"Well . . . ," Goldenrod began and then paused. She still hadn't told anyone about the map, not even in her phone call the night before to Charla, because she wanted the final product to be a big surprise. She had considered telling Birch, but then she was sure he would want to help—and even though having an assistant to aid with the measurements would be a huge time-saver, babysitting a little brother was definitely the opposite of an adventure; Meriwether Lewis certainly hadn't brought his along.

But there was something about the old woman, some funny way in which she stood stooped there, waiting with bated breath to see what Goldenrod would say, that made Goldenrod want to trust her. "I'm making a map, actually."

"A map?" the woman asked.

"Yup. It's going to be the most accurate map of Pilmilton in the world. Every house. Every tree. Every shrub. Everything."

"Wonderful!" the woman exclaimed. "What a splendid idea."

"Thanks." Goldenrod smiled.

"What are you going to do first?"

"Well . . . I think I'll get a rough sketch of your house and this area."

"And what will you do after that?"

"Take a few measurements. Make sure everything is drawn to scale," Goldenrod said.

"And after?"

"Then I'll have to go into the woods. That'll be the hardest part, I think, what with all the trees . . ."

"I was hoping you'd say that! Are you really going into the woods?" the woman asked.

Goldenrod nodded.

"Is there any way you could do me a tiny favor?"

"What is it?" Goldenrod held her sketchbook limply at her side, all but forgotten at this point.

"Well, at the very center of the woods, there is a certain bush, a rosebush. And it blooms very, very rarely: for three days only, once every fifty years. It blooms with the most magnificent rose you've ever seen. It's a bright, bright shade of blue and smells just like a summer night."

"What does a summer night smell like?"

"I can't explain it, but if you smell this rose, you'll know immediately what I mean. Anyway, I'm sure this bush is pretty rare. I've seen a lot of roses, and I've never seen anything like it." The old lady glanced knowingly at Goldenrod and her own admittedly spectacular rose garden before continuing. "I have calculated that this bush is set to bloom Monday, Tuesday, and Wednesday of next week. And then that will be the last time it will bloom for half a century. I had planned to go in myself, you see, but, well . . ." The woman sighed deeply.

"What?" Goldenrod asked a little breathlessly.

"Well. You may have noticed, I'm pretty old."

Goldenrod didn't know what to say. Would it be rude to agree with her or rude not to? In the end, she decided to side with the truth and nodded. The old woman laughed, flashing her hideous teeth.

"With my arthritis, I think it'll take me about a week just to make it to the center of the woods. And if I'm gone for a week, believe me, my son will have the whole town out looking for me. Then I'll be the crazy old lady on the news who dodged a search party and claimed I was only trying to pluck a rose."

Goldenrod hesitated for a moment. "Why don't you just take a cell phone in there with you?"

"Smart girl! Unfortunately, can't get any reception in the woods. See how dense those trees are?" She pointed to them.

Uh-oh, Goldenrod thought. *No reception?* Well, she couldn't see any reason why her mother would have to know about that.

"Can't you just tell your son where you're going and then he won't worry?"

The old woman laughed again. "You just wait until your seventy-one-year-old mother tells you she's planning to hike all alone into the woods and see what you say!"

Seventy-one? Goldenrod would have guessed that she was more like a hundred. But that was probably the fairy tales talking again.

"I haven't dared mention this whole rose idea to any-one," the old lady continued. "In fact, you're the only person I've ever told about it."

"Really? Why would you tell me?" Goldenrod blinked in surprise.

"Same reason I'm the only one you ever told about your map."

"But how did you—"

"You just wait until you're seventy-one, honey. You'd be surprised the amount of things you know. Anyway, since you're already on your way into the woods, if you run across that bush next week, could you cut three roses for me? They will keep for a whole week if you're able to store them in an airtight container as soon as you clip them," the old lady continued, her eyes shining almost as if she could see Goldenrod's specimen jar through her backpack.

"Sure," Goldenrod said without any hesitation. Flora that possibly no one had ever heard of before? This was clearly a great stroke of luck!

"Wonderful! Thank you so much. And just for even saying you'll try, how about I help you out with some of those measurements? It seems like you could save time if you had an assistant, eh?"

Goldenrod had no idea how the old woman knew what she had been thinking, but she was glad for the help. So she took out her measuring tape, gave one end to the old lady, and went about the business of measuring all around her house. For a brief, shining moment she wondered if maybe this old lady would turn into her replacement Clark. But then she came to her senses and remembered the woman's arthritis and why she couldn't go into the woods in the first place. Still, there was something about this old lady that Goldenrod liked very much, and that afternoon, for the first time in a while, she felt like she was talking to someone just like she would to a friend.

INTO THE WOODS

The next day, Goldenrod was ready to finally step into the forest itself. As soon as she arrived at its edge, she saw the old lady again diligently working in her garden.

"How about a muffin before you set off?" the old lady asked her.

Goldenrod hesitated and took a quick peek at her watch.

"I'll make it snappy," the old lady promised.

"Sure. Thank you," Goldenrod said.

"Just have a seat." She pointed to one of two rusty white metal chairs on her front porch before she bustled into the house.

She was back a minute later, carrying a plastic store-bought bin of muffins and two mugs with spoons sticking out of them. "Nothing goes better with banana chocolate chip muffins than chocolate milk."

"Thank you," Goldenrod said politely as she stared at the chalky mixture inside her mug. A big clump of powder floated on top, and Goldenrod set to work on it with the spoon.

"You know, you really do have an amazing rose garden. I bet my mother would love to see it," Goldenrod said.

"Oh? Is she a gardener?"

"She's obsessed."

"How wonderful." The old lady sighed.

They spent a few more minutes discussing some of the finer points of Mrs. Moram's garden while Goldenrod picked at her stale muffin and drank most of her chocolate milk.

"I should get going," Goldenrod eventually said.

"Of course, of course. You have very important work to do," the old lady said without a single note of sarcasm.

Goldenrod smiled as she took her backpack. "See you later," she said and headed toward the forest.

She had only walked a few steps in when she noticed right away how different the forest felt from anywhere else she'd ever been. The first thing she observed was the light. Almost immediately, the trees above her closed in, creating a dense green and gold roof that filtered the sunlight in an almost magical way. The entire world was bathed in a soft glow with the trees themselves rustling gently and reminding Goldenrod of gossiping ladies leaning into each other. The ground was a richer shade of brown, and Goldenrod could see patches of emerald-green moss growing in certain places.

And then there were the sounds, because, surprisingly, the woods were very noisy: not in a traffic-on-the-street, kids-on-a-playground way but in a did-you-ever-know-there-were-so-many-species-of-birds way. Maybe one of those birds, Goldenrod thought excitedly, would not be found in Charla's *Encyclopedia of North American Flora and Fauna*. Maybe one of them was just waiting to be discovered by her. She wondered for a moment whether if she did discover a new species, it would be named after her, like Lewis's Woodpecker was named after him.

Goldenrod allowed herself another five minutes to soak in the surreal beauty of the woods and the grandiose thoughts of her future as a famous explorer, before making herself get back to work. She backtracked so that she was once again at the edge of the forest and then took out her sketchbook and her new and improved measuring tape. She had spent the night before working on it, so that now the end of the tape had a hole punched out of it that was the perfect size for one of Mr. Moram's golf tees. By using the tee as a stake in the ground, Goldenrod could easily and quickly measure things as a solo explorer.

The morning went along quietly enough, and by late afternoon, Goldenrod had made a sizable amount of progress measuring distances and documenting a few insects as

she came across them. She was just about to try and draw a
rather large, purplish one when she heard something. It wasn't
a buzzing or a chirping or a croaking; in fact, it didn't sound
like a noise any bug or animal would make at all. What it
sounded like . . . was a laugh.

She looked up from her work and listened more
intently. This time, after a few moments, she heard a rustling. It sounded like it was coming from a southeasterly
direction and like it was getting farther away.

Goldenrod sprang up to investigate. She followed the
rustling sound as best she could until, after a couple of minutes, she found herself entering a small, almost perfectly cir-
cular clearing. She listened for the rustling noise again to see
where to go next. She waited. But after about ten minutes,
when all she could make out were the normal chirping and
cawing sounds she had grown used to over the past few
hours, she realized she had lost the trail.

She took a look around the little clearing and figured she
would make her way back there—methodically speaking—in
a couple of days' time to map it. She waited just a few more
minutes to make sure that the noise wouldn't start up again,
thinking that it might be a small animal and hoping that
she would come across it later. *Perhaps a small animal with an
unusual call*, Goldenrod thought, as she once again heard what
sounded like a very far-off giggle.

Too bad she didn't have more time to investigate today,

she realized as she looked at her watch and saw that it was almost 5:20 p.m. already. She found her way back out of the forest again, gave the old lady a wave as she passed her by, and headed home—feeling confident about her chances of a great forest discovery after all.

THE TRANSPARENT MAN

When Goldenrod went downstairs at precisely 9:00 a.m. the next day to set out for the forest, Birch was waiting for her at the front door. He eyed her green backpack curiously.

"Morning," Goldenrod said.

"Hi," Birch said and then hesitated. "Where are you going?"

"Oh . . . just around town."

"Why?"

Goldenrod shrugged. "Exercise, fresh air, that sort of thing."

"You sound like a grown-up," Birch said.

"Do I?" Goldenrod asked. She *was* feeling a little bit taller these days.

Birch shrugged and then finally asked, "Can I come?"

Goldenrod sighed. It was one of those questions she had

been dreading because she knew how much Birch looked up to her. In all honesty, most of the time, she really liked having him around, but this was just one thing she felt she had to do on her own. She was genuinely sorry when she told him no.

Birch didn't cause a scene but quietly walked away. It didn't feel so great to make her little brother sad.

She felt better when she was closer to the forest, though, and especially as she gave a jaunty wave to the old lady before heading in.

She picked up where she had left off the day before and soon finished another small section on her grid. Now she had to decide which way to go. Since she had gone southeast toward the little clearing the day before, she decided that maybe she would give northeast a try. She picked up her backpack and was heading in that direction when she heard a tiny cough.

She stopped and turned around. The forest was making its usual forest sounds, but she didn't see a single creature in sight that she thought could cough in that way.

After another minute of making sure the coast was totally clear, she walked a little farther northeast.

Ahem.

There it was again. And this time it was much louder and unmistakably the sound of someone clearing their throat.

Goldenrod looked all around her once more, but absolutely no one was there. If Birch's "grown-up" comment hadn't been still fresh in her mind, she might have felt a tiny bit nervous. *Explorers don't get scared though,* she thought. *They figure out what's going on.*

She stayed put for one minute, two. When she was certain that there really was no one else besides herself, she put her foot one step in the direction she was going.

"Well, really. You are going the wrong way, you know," a polite voice said from behind her.

Goldenrod whipped around.

Standing there was a tall, elegant man. He was dressed in very old-fashioned clothing: a maroon coat with tails, a beige scarf around his neck, tan pants, and high brown boots, and he leaned on a thin, elegant cane. He had gray hair, though his face looked pretty young and unlined with its long nose and small blue eyes. But perhaps the most extraordinary thing about him was that he was rather transparent.

To her surprise, and probably the man's, Goldenrod actually found herself quite calm. In fact, the first words out of her mouth were, "Wrong way for what?"

"Your quest, of course," the tall, transparent man said with a smile.

The two stared at each other. Finally, after another few moments of study, Goldenrod spoke again. "Do I know you?"

"You might. Or you might not. It's hard for me to keep up with the state of the education system these days," the man said.

Goldenrod continued to stare. She was certain that the man's face was familiar.

"I must say," he went on, "I am rather impressed with how splendidly you are handling my appearance. Then again, I supposed you would handle it that way if you were the right man—excuse me, the right girl—for the job."

"Are you—"

In a flash, the man was gone.

Goldenrod stared and stared at the spot where he had been. She sat down right on the forest floor and leaned against a tree. There was certainly no tall, elegant see-through man there now. But there almost certainly had been just a moment ago.

She looked at all of her very scientific notes and her very scientific tools (well, minus the yellow sock). She went through how logically her day had gone until then. Cornflakes and bananas for breakfast. A kiss from her mother. A conversation with her brother in which she had to assert her older sister status. And then her map going precisely as planned. She was an explorer, a scientist. What she had just thought she'd seen was quite impossible. And yet, she was almost positive she had seen it.

Goldenrod didn't get much accomplished the rest of the day. After a bit more thinking, and a written documentation of what had just happened in her Explorer's Journal (the lined notebook), Goldenrod found that she couldn't concentrate enough on the detailed measurements.

Around three, she left the forest with the hope that she would see the old lady on her way out. She thought that if there were anyone at all whom she could discuss her strange experience with, it would be her.

But the old lady was nowhere to be found. Goldenrod even went so far as to knock on her door, but got no answer.

Stuck with the disconcerting idea that she didn't know whether to believe her own eyes, Goldenrod had no choice but to go home.

✳

The man from the forest was staring at Goldenrod.

On a strong hunch, she had gone quickly to her room as soon as she had gotten home and pulled out her own copy of the Lewis and Clark biography. Right there, on page nineteen, was a portrait captioned "Meriwether Lewis." A portrait that depicted the same gray hair and clear blue eyes that she'd seen, though positioned on a face that seemed rather more solid.

BOREDOM AND CURIOSITY

Birch was bored. Nearly three weeks had passed since second grade ended and in those three weeks he had beaten all of his video games, perfected mimicking the voices of every single one of his favorite cartoon characters, and tried every possible variation of Goldenrod's peanut butter sandwich that he could think of. His last concoction of peanut butter, chili powder, and raw egg had left a very bad taste in his mouth, literally, and now his stomach gurgled in protest any time he got too close to the kitchen.

So now he was bored. And he missed Goldenrod. Every morning, precisely at 9:00 a.m., he watched as she set out with her green backpack, and every evening, at around 6:00 p.m., he watched as she walked back toward the house. When she had turned down his request to go with her, he hadn't been particularly surprised. After all, the world as he knew it definitely involved an older sister's right not to bring her eight-year-old brother along everywhere she went. He didn't necessarily like it, but he hadn't asked her again.

But, really, boredom can make a person do all sorts of things one would probably never do otherwise. Suddenly, one finds oneself acting mean or loud or absolutely, monstrously bonkers simply because one doesn't have anything better to do. In Birch's case, boredom had wormed its way into his head and made him act very un-Birchlike indeed.

Whatever Goldenrod is doing, he thought one day, *it has to be more fun than this*. And then, suddenly, he had decided that he wasn't going to stand for it anymore. Take note, boredom. This was war.

At 8:00 a.m. that very next morning, Birch took his own purple-and-gold backpack and filled it with a notebook, a box of colored pencils, and the brand-new calculator he had received on his last birthday. He stashed the bag under his bed. Then he took out a Tupperware he had specially prepared the night before. Inside was a particularly odorous mixture of peanut butter, one raw egg, and a mashed can of chili beans. Now that it had settled in overnight, the gooey green-and-brown concoction looked—and smelled— perfect for his plans.

Still in his pajamas, Birch walked into the bathroom and proceeded to scoop out the goo all over the tiles closest to the toilet. He sculpted the mixture with the spoon to get it just right and then ran back to his room to hide the Tupperware. Within a few moments, he was back in the bathroom, performing a few convincing coughs and barfing noises, and then finally screaming "Mom!" in his best weak-with-dire-illness voice.

When his mother came, she found Birch grabbing his stomach and looking miserably at the mess on the floor. "I'm sorry," he managed to say weakly before bringing his hand to his mouth.

Exactly as he had expected, Birch was led back to his bed, a thermometer was produced, and he was ordered to take a nap. While his mother cleaned the mess, he closed his eyes and steadied his breathing so that, when she came in to check on him at 8:45 a.m., he looked every bit like a sick little boy fast asleep.

At 8:55 a.m., on the other hand, Birch looked every bit like a determined boy with a very serious mission. Crouched behind the hydrangea bushes in his backyard, wearing an all-green outfit, his camouflage baseball hat and his purple-and-gold backpack cleverly tucked under a hoodie, he waited until he had heard Goldenrod say good-bye to their mother and then make her way down the road.

Then, as his mother pruned, he tiptoed out from behind the bush, quietly opened the gate, and briskly followed Goldenrod's path.

For a week, Goldenrod had diligently mapped out Pilmilton Woods without further incident and found nothing to indicate that there had ever been any ghosts there, famous or otherwise.

For at least a day or two after their first encounter, she had been on the lookout for Meriwether Lewis. She had headed toward the little clearing that she'd been led to by that small laugh. "Hello?" she'd called out, a little tentatively. The birds chirped and the sun shone, but it had still been a tiny bit intimidating to bait a ghost, even if the ghost was the spirit of one of her all-time heroes.

It turned out that she didn't really have to worry; there was no answer. She had called his name some more. She had tried walking in the "wrong direction" as before, hoping this would cause the ghost to come out and tell her so. She had even once said, "I'm on a quest" loudly, thinking those might be the magic words that would make him appear. But they had merely echoed off of the trees and sounded rather bizarre, even to herself.

Eventually she had given up and returned to her map. By the end of the week, the effect of all her very precise measuring and her scientific documentation was this: she had started to doubt that she'd ever seen the ghost at all.

Could it just be that she had been tired, fallen asleep in the forest, and had a very vivid dream? Really, were there even such things as ghosts? And if there were, what would be the probability that Meriwether Lewis would choose dinky Pilmilton to haunt, anyway?

Very slim, she had to answer for herself, because the only two people she could think of to tell about the whole thing were the old lady and Charla—the first of whom she hadn't seen for a week and the second of whom she hadn't seen for much longer, and couldn't find the right words to type in an e-mail to her and not sound pretty crazy anyway.

But even though she hadn't seen the old lady again, Goldenrod hadn't forgotten her promise to clip three blue roses for her—and the delicious thought that a new discovery just might await her. She had her specimen jar and her shears ready. The only problem was that she had yet to come across any such rosebush.

And soon enough, according to the old lady's calculation, it came to be the last day that the rosebush would bloom for fifty years. Goldenrod had decided to spend most of it laying aside her accurate map (and any lingering thoughts of transparent men) in favor of pure exploration. Knowing she still had to be precise with the ground she covered, though, she went deeper into the forest, using her grid system as a guide. She had just about finished a thorough examination of the first unmapped square on her grid when she got a glimpse of a deep blue something through a clump of trees.

Her heart leaped with excitement, but it only lasted a moment before she realized that the blue thing she was seeing was moving and that hovering somewhere above it was a sweaty white T-shirt.

No matter how unusual this blue rose might have been, it seemed unlikely that it would be mobile and wearing clothing. It also didn't seem very probable that an animal like a coyote or a prairie dog or a pygmy short-horned lizard—all of which had been discovered by Lewis and Clark—would be found wearing a sweaty white T-shirt in its natural habitat. *But then again*, thought Goldenrod, *one must never jump to conclusions without full exploration if one wants to be a true pioneer.*

Goldenrod quietly started to run after the flashing white T-shirt and blue jeans. It wasn't too hard to follow, since whomever the shirt belonged to was not very stealthy. The snapping branches and startled bird sounds were enough to ensure Goldenrod that she was both on the right track and had little chance of being overheard.

A couple of minutes later, the sound of broken twigs was replaced by a girl's voice. "There you are, Lint. What took you so long?"

"The security guard was watching me," Sweaty T-shirt Guy panted. And Goldenrod realized she knew that voice.

"But you weren't doing anything suspicious, were you?" She knew the third voice too.

Goldenrod tiptoed behind a tree to get a better look. There were Charlie Cookman and Jonas Levins, looking as mean as they ever had in school, right in the middle of her forest.

CAN'T REWIND

Charlie and Jonas weren't alone. With them was an older girl with dirty-blond hair whom Goldenrod didn't recognize.

"I was just drawing," Charlie said.

"Well, did you get everything done?" the girl spoke again. She looked about twelve or thirteen. There were patches of dirt on her face, and her hair seemed to be matted from grease.

Charlie pulled some things from his pockets. Goldenrod could make out a crumpled piece of gridded paper with what looked like a detailed diagram on it. To her great surprise, it almost looked like it could be a map of some sort.

"That's it?" the girl asked.

"I told you, that security guard knew I was up to something. I had to get out of there fast," Charlie said.

The girl turned to Jonas. "Look, Brains. Why don't you live up to your name a little and not send the dumb kid to do the job where, you know, you need to act like you belong in a museum."

"I'm not dumb!" Charlie said as he rolled up his T-shirt and started to fuss around with his cavernous belly button, around which there were muscles for miles.

"Right. And I'm not a girl. And Brains is an idiot. Although I'm starting to suspect . . ."

"Stupid girl," Charlie muttered.

"Sorry? What did you say?"

"Better to send me than a girl," Charlie said as he continued to pull bits and pieces of things from his belly button and quickly transfer them to his right-hand pocket.

"And why is that, Lint?" The girl's voice had become soft and dangerous.

"'Cause you'd probably cry."

"Wow, my gosh. You're totally right. I'm a *girl* so I just couldn't handle the ninety-seven-year-old security guard that you can barely outsmart. If only your brain was as big as your biceps."

Charlie took a moment before he responded again with, "Stupid girl."

The girl casually brought her index finger to the side of her nose, tilted her head up, took a deep breath, and exhaled quickly to land a large booger squarely on the side of Charlie's head.

"Ugh!" Charlie yelled as he went to wipe it off. "I'm gonna—"

"What? What are you going to do?" the girl asked.

"All right, that's enough." Jonas finally stepped in. "Honestly, Snotshot. Do you have to do that every time?"

"You need to get some more useful friends, Brains."

"Look, Lint's done a good job casing the place. The camera diagram is almost finished, and I'll get No-Bone to finish the rest today. Was there anything else, Lint?"

"Yeah, I got us some food," Charlie—for some reason apparently also called Lint—said slowly. He took out a few silver-wrapped rectangles from his pocket.

"Oh, ew. Not those protein bars again. The only one who likes those things is you, Lint," the girl called Snotshot said.

"It's peanut butter chocolate . . . ," Lint started.

"No, it's not. It's mildly peanut-butter-and-chocolate-flavored cardboard. Do you understand that the whole point of having the food schedule is so we all get something *everyone* wants to eat?" She turned to Jonas. "Do I seriously need to explain everything to him? Shouldn't that be your job, *Brains*?"

"All right, all right," Jonas—or did that girl just call him Brains?—said sharply before turning to Charlie again. "Thanks for the diagram, Lint. And, for the record, I don't mind the energy bars."

Lint smiled smugly at the girl, who rolled her eyes and

turned to Brains. "This whole thing had better work. Spit-bubble is getting impatient."

"I know exactly how Spitbubble is feeling. Thanks," Brains said coldly.

Spitbubble? Seriously? Goldenrod thought. Her own name was starting to sound more and more normal with each passing moment. Positively generic, even.

"Wait, did you hear that?" Lint asked.

Goldenrod had heard it too: the sound of footsteps snapping twigs. And they weren't hers.

She saw him before they did, an unusually small boy dressed in camouflage clothing and carrying a purple-and-gold backpack. He had walked smack into the clearing where the four older kids stood.

"Who is that?" Snotshot asked.

"Isn't that Mold-and-rot's little brother?" Brains asked.

"Who's Mold-and-rot?" Snotshot asked.

"Some girl in our class," Lint answered.

Brains was already going up to Birch, who seemed just as surprised to see them as they were to see him. He was trying to slowly back away into the forest, as if that would somehow rewind time and make the older kids forget they had ever laid eyes on him.

"What are you doing here, kid?" Brains asked.

"Nothing," Birch managed to reply.

"What did you hear?" Brains asked.

"Nothing. I was just . . . lost."

"We'd better take him to Spitbubble," the girl said. "He'd want to know about someone snooping around."

"Spitbubble won't want this kid," Brains replied. "He has a family. A real one."

"Still, he'll want to decide what to do with him."

Brains sighed. "All right. But let's go quickly. The last thing we need is a search party of Morams finding us. Lint, grab him, and let's go back to Headquarters."

Lint stepped forward and swallowed Birch's tiny wrist in his fist. "Come on," he said roughly.

The three older kids started to lead Birch away. Snotshot walked last, allowing her to expertly open up Birch's backpack without anyone else noticing. She started to remove Birch's belongings one by one.

Goldenrod was paralyzed. A series of questions seemed to be replaying in her head at warp speed. Most of them went something like, where on earth had Birch come from? Or, how had their mother let him leave the house? As she watched the four kids go deeper into the forest, she finally felt herself becoming unglued from her spot. Those were questions she was just going to have to deal with later. Right now, she needed to figure out how to save her little brother.

DOWN, DOWN, DOWN

With no real plan, Goldenrod followed Birch and his captors from as far behind as she could without losing them. They were heading deep into the forest, to places Goldenrod probably wouldn't have even reached for at least a week. The kids weren't talking much. All Goldenrod could hear were the sounds of twigs breaking beneath their feet and of Charlie's heavy breathing. Birch wasn't making a sound, wasn't even crying, and Goldenrod found herself both surprised and proud of him.

The trees were getting denser here, and the day seemed to be going in fast-forward as the closely knit leaves made everything grow darker and darker. Goldenrod tripped on an especially large tree root and fell into a big and crunchy shrub; she froze, certain that the group ahead must have heard her. But after a few moments, as their footsteps were still fading farther away, she decided it was safe to get back up and continue following them. It wasn't easy. The minute she'd lost had also caused her to lose sight of them, and she had to rely on the sound of sneakers on snapping twigs. Straining her ears, she proceeded ahead, unsure of where she was and whether she was still on the right track.

Suddenly, Goldenrod couldn't hear footsteps anymore, and she started to worry that she had lost them. She listened intently but . . . nothing. She looked around where she stood, but all she could see were trees. Beautiful, enormous, silent trees that could tell her nothing about the whereabouts of her brother.

Goldenrod realized she had gone about this all wrong and way too hastily. She needed to retrace her steps. But first, she needed to figure out where she was. She opened her backpack and took out her compass. She watched the little golden arrow inside it spin and point north for her. At least now, if nothing else, she knew that she was facing northeast.

"It appears as if you've lost something," a polite voice said.

Goldenrod looked up sharply. There, leaning on his cane, was the transparent man.

❋

Birch's wrist hurt. He was rubbing it as he stood in an odd stone entrance in the middle of the forest. As far as he could tell, he was inside a giant boulder, and a crude stone

staircase lay a few feet in front of him. The stone walls of
the staircase held flashlights that were taped on with massive amounts of duct tape. They were making long, oddly
shaped shadows on the walls.

His captors were whispering behind him. Birch recognized the big kid and his friend who had tried to mess with
him and gotten Goldenrod in trouble on the last day of
school. He didn't remember their real names, but he had
found out pretty quickly that they were called Lint and Brains
here. The blond girl, Snotshot, he'd never seen before in his
life.

Birch could tell they didn't know what to do with him.
Whoever Spitbubble was, he wasn't here, and this was causing a problem. The girl kept insisting that they keep Birch,
but Brains was arguing against it. Birch found himself silently
rooting for Brains.

He was surprisingly calm, which surprised himself most
of all. He guessed it had something to do with being in
shock. Although he didn't think the older kids would necessarily hurt him, he was worried about his mother. He
should be getting back pretty soon if he didn't want her to
know he was gone. He would be in major trouble if she
found out he had left at all, but what would she do if she discovered he had left . . . and hadn't come back?

I could run, he thought, as he saw a perfect Birch-sized
gap between the entrance and where the older kids stood.
But how far would he get? That girl looked fast. Still, it was

better than hanging around here and doing nothing. But just as he was about to summon up the courage to make a break for it, his window of opportunity got eclipsed by two other boys who joined his original three captors.

The first new kid looked dirtier than the others, but underneath the dirt, Birch could tell he had curly hair and was dressed in nice clothes. Expensive clothes with a certain monkey logo that his mother had said they couldn't afford to get for him last year. The other new kid was older and probably taller, though it was hard for Birch to tell because he was folded over like an accordion.

"What's going on here?" the bendy kid asked. "Who is that shrimp?" He pointed toward Birch.

"Mold-and-rot's brother," Lint said.

"Whoa, really?" the kid with the blue-monkey-logo shirt said.

"What do you think, Toe Jam?" Snotshot asked as she turned around to look at the kid in the blue T-shirt. "Brains and Lint here want to let him go back home. But I say we oughta keep him until Spitbubble knows the situation. No-Bone, you agree with me, right?"

The bendy kid nodded, his spine doing an awful yet fascinating jig along with his head.

"All I'm saying," Brains started, "is that if we leave him here, he's going to have parents looking for him. And I'm sure no one wants that. Least of all Spitbubble."

"So what are we going to do? Just have him pinkie swear

that he won't tell anybody and send him away?" Snotshot snapped.

"He doesn't know anything!" Brains replied.

"Toe Jam. You're breaking our tie," Snotshot said. "Should he stay or do we send him straight back to Mommy where he can immediately tell the entire town everything he's seen and heard here today?" She folded her arms defiantly.

Toe Jam looked up eagerly at her. "I think Snotshot's right," he said, his voice a little squeaky.

"Well, of course he would agree. The idiot's in love with you," Brains said angrily.

Toe Jam turned beet red. "I am not!"

But Snotshot looked pretty smug. "It's a vote fair and square. Three to two."

"Fine," Brains said. "Then you guys figure out where you're gonna be keeping him. I'm staying out of this."

"Oh, really? And you'd like me to tell Spitbubble what, exactly, when he finds out you're not helping?" Snotshot said.

"I'm not scared of you," Brains said.

"And Spitbubble?"

"I'm not scared of him either," Brains said, but much less convincingly.

Snotshot made a very loud snorting noise, louder and more impressive than Birch had ever heard anyone make in his whole life.

Despite what he had said about not getting involved, Brains was now coming toward him. He grabbed Birch by the wrist. "Come on. Lint, follow me."

Lint walked behind, as Brains led Birch past the entrance-way and down, down, down.

GHOSTS AND BUTLERS

It's you," Goldenrod said breathlessly to the transparent man.

"It usually is," he replied calmly, walking toward her. Goldenrod noticed that he had a slight limp.

She had to ask. "Are you . . . Meriwether Lewis?"

The man gave a little bow. "Indeed, I am. Or I was. Well, I'm his spirit, anyway."

"But there are no such things as ghosts," Goldenrod muttered.

"Who told you that?" the spirit of Meriwether Lewis asked.

"My parents, mainly," Goldenrod confessed, thinking specifically of that one summer when she was six and had spent a great deal of nights asking to sleep in her parents' room.

"And they are grown-ups, I assume?" the man asked. Goldenrod nodded.

"Unfortunately, it has come to my attention that the modern world is sorely lacking in imagination. And grown-ups are the biggest culprits of all. Regardless, the simple fact is, here I am. And seeing how I was born in 1774, I can't very well *not* be a ghost, now can I?"

"I guess not," Goldenrod said.

"Very well. Now that we've established that, let's move on. So I suppose you were the one who was sent on the quest."

"The quest?"

"To claim our lost discovery: the blue rose."

"Oh, *that* quest," Goldenrod said, faintly starting to grasp some of what was going on.

"Do you have any other quests going on at the moment?" Meriwether Lewis asked politely.

"No, no. The old lady told me about the rose but . . . well, I thought she just wanted it for her garden." A thought struck Goldenrod, and she eyed the ghost suspiciously. "Wait, does she know you're here?"

Meriwether Lewis shrugged. "I'm afraid I don't know much about what goes on outside of this forest. My spirit is trapped here, you see, until the blue rose can take its right-ful place as discovered flora."

A smile slowly crept its way up Goldenrod's face. She

was completely spellbound. It's not often that one gets to meet someone one has read about admiringly, and it's even less likely when said person has been dead for hundreds of years. But beyond that, this man—or spirit—was speaking her language. He was telling her that her initial excitement over the blue rose was well founded.

It took a few seconds for Goldenrod to remember what had just happened to her little brother. "Oh!" she said, startling herself out of her own reverie. "This is all so interesting, Mr. Lewis—"

"Please. Call me Meriwether."

"Meriwether. Yes, this is fascinating and, believe me, I would love nothing better than to find this blue rose, but right now, I have to go rescue my little brother. He's been kidnapped."

"Ah," Meriwether said, as if this sort of thing happened all the time. Though maybe if you were a ghost haunting a forest for two centuries, nothing much fazed you. "Your little brother. Of course. And, is he your Clark?"

"Well . . . no," Goldenrod said. "Not really. I suppose my friend Charla is. But he's important all the same."

"Of course, of course," Meriwether said. "Well, if it's a kidnapping that's happened, I have a good idea who might be responsible."

At that, he perked up a little and held his hand to his ear. "And I think there's something over there that you may want to pay attention to." He pointed to a faraway grove of trees where Goldenrod saw another flash of white.

When she turned back to Meriwether, he was gone. Trying hard to focus on the task at hand instead of replaying the ultraexciting conversation she had just had, Goldenrod headed quickly over to the trees. Through them, she glimpsed a man walking briskly.

The man had salt-and-pepper hair and wore a black suit. It was the crisp white shirt underneath this suit that had caught Goldenrod's eye. With no other leads anywhere in sight, Goldenrod decided to take Meriwether's advice. She started to follow the man in the suit.

He was a tallish man and took long strides that Goldenrod had trouble keeping up with. He seemed almost businesslike as he marched on toward his destination.

Goldenrod still had her compass out and could see that they were now walking through parts of the woods where she had never been before. They were heading on a much different path than the one Goldenrod had chased Charlie, Jonas, and company through. For a moment, she considered turning back and retracing her steps. But then she made a firm decision to trust Meriwether who, ghost or not, was still one of the bravest and greatest explorers who had ever lived. If nothing else, the man had to have a good sense of direction.

It must have been at least twenty minutes later that the

man in the black suit finally stopped. He was standing right next to a bush that was covered with tiny, hard red berries. He waited there.

Goldenrod was well concealed behind some other bushes and knew the man couldn't see her. She wondered if she should go talk to him and explain her situation. Maybe he could help. On the other hand, Meriwether hadn't expressly advised her to do so, and her own instincts were telling her that maybe talking to a stranger deep in the middle of an unmapped forest was not the best idea in the world.

While Goldenrod was brewing over this dilemma, she heard a voice.

"Do you have it?" the voice asked, slightly impatiently.

Goldenrod peered through the bushes and could make out a dirty blue shirt and a tuft of curly hair in between the trees.

The man took out a slim plastic case from his pocket.

"Are you sure, Master Randy, that you really want this? This coin has been in your family for practically two centuries."

Goldenrod almost gasped. That tuft of curly hair and extremely dirty blue shirt belonged to another classmate of hers: Randy S. Lewis-O'Malley to be precise, probably the richest kid in school, chauffeured limos to drop him off in the morning and all. But just what was he doing here and why was he so filthy?

"Toulouse, how many times have I told you not to question my authority?" Randy hissed.

"Not quite as many times as your father has told me to question your every move, Toe Jam," Toulouse answered calmly.

Randy glared. "Yes, he cares *so* much that he lets his second-favorite butler keep me in line."

Toulouse looked unmoved.

"Gimme the coin," Randy said. Toulouse handed him the case.

Randy opened it and rubbed one grimy hand over the coin, which caught the light and flashed a brilliant gold that matched the dappled sunlight on the surrounding trees. Goldenrod could see Toulouse cringe.

"That is all for now," Randy said.

"You will not need Cook's services?"

"The other kids are tired of all that fancy food. None of them even know what Camembert is . . ."

"Shocking turn of events," Toulouse muttered.

Randy squinted his eyes. "Anyway, no. That is all."

Toulouse nodded and turned smartly back in the direction from where he had come. Goldenrod had to duck quickly behind the bush she was in to avoid being seen. Luckily, it seemed Toulouse was too busy focusing on maintaining the excruciating poise of an excellent butler to notice that a seemingly ordinary bush had sprouted a long, brown ponytail.

Randy, meanwhile, had turned around and was saun-
tering back in the opposite direction.

"Follow him," a polite voice whispered near Goldenrod's ear.

BOOMING VOICES

Toe Jam rubbed the large gold coin in his hand as he made his way back to the cavern. He loved to grime up the shiny, immaculate things that came from his shiny, immaculate house. Back at home, his parents would freak if everything wasn't perfectly spotless and in its place. But here in the forest, he could be as dirty and gross as he wanted to be, and there was no one to scold him for it. In fact, being dirty and gross was encouraged here. That's how Spitbubble would pick what nickname to bestow upon them, and that's how each of them knew that they really belonged.

He smirked as he thought of the impressive collection of sock fuzz that he had picked from in between his toes and that was just waiting to be discovered in his top dresser drawer. He had really had to scramble to come up with a hobby worthy of the Gross-Out Gang, but he was pretty proud of his final choice, after ruling out things like trying to grow his nose hair (which would take way too long) or eating gas-inducing beans for every meal (which were vegetables and, therefore, inherently wrong). The maid had probably gotten rid of his toe jam collection by now, but he could always restock when he got back home.

Toe Jam had spent all of his considerable January and February allowance to bribe Toulouse into telling his parents that he was spending yet another summer at sleepaway camp. Instead he was happily hidden away here, in a forest not five miles from his mansion. He couldn't help but suspect that his parents were also more than a little pleased to have a break from the one thing in their lives that was the hardest to keep clean.

Meanwhile, he was having the summer of his life. For the first time, he felt like he belonged somewhere his parents hadn't paid to get him into. Well, at least they didn't know they had paid, Toe Jam thought as he looked at the slightly dulled coin. The other kids should be pretty impressed by this. Maybe even Snotshot.

He could feel his cheeks flush a little as he thought about her and was glad no one was around to see it, even though the dirt on his face probably concealed it anyway. The thing was, he didn't really *like* like Snotshot or anything. It was just that he thought she could be kinda cool and was maybe a little pretty. When she wasn't shooting boogers at people, of course.

Then again, Toe Jam smiled a little to himself, if he had to be perfectly honest, that was probably one of the coolest things about her.

※

The cavern was surprisingly large, Birch thought, as he continued to walk in between Brains and Lint. They had made their way down the "stairs" and were now in an extremely long underground hallway. The stone walls were pockmarked and slightly slanted, making it obvious that the structure was a hundred percent naturally made.

Birch was trying to keep his mind occupied to distract it from the sheer panic that was itching to spring up. He was observing his surroundings very carefully and was surprised to walk by a pile of unmade sheets and pillows. The makeshift bed, he noted, was inside one of a few little "rooms" he was passing, and each one of them seemed to be filled with belongings, like clothes and backpacks. One was even painted a pale shade of slime green. Another had faded posters on the walls.

There were little hallways everywhere. Birch thought they could have been escape routes, but then he realized that he had absolutely no idea where those escape routes would lead. They could land him in an even bigger pickle than the one he was already in, so he immediately forced his mind to change the subject. Since it had already wandered to the subject of pickles, he started to concoct sandwich combinations in his head.

He was just about to put the top slice of toast on his imaginary sausage, Swiss, pickle, and barbecue-sauce sandwich when Brains grunted, "We're here."

"Here" was another small room off of the main hallway. This one was bare except for some scattered rocks and a flashlight taped to the wall, which Brains switched on.

Brains pointed at the floor. "Sit down. You're going to stay here. Quietly. Got it?"

Birch nodded and slowly lowered himself.

"Hold on," Brains said and walked out of the room. A few moments later, he was back with a small pillow. "Here. The ground's hard."

"Thanks," Birch said softly and repositioned himself so that he was sitting on the pillow. The ground was warm and he could hear a very faint gurgling sound coming from underneath it, almost like running water.

Brains then turned to Lint. "You are not to leave that front door. Got it? Not if you get hungry, tired, bored, I don't care. You don't leave until someone comes down to take over."

"Yeah, yeah," Lint said glumly. "How come I get all the cruddy jobs?"

"Guarding this kid's about the most important job we've got right now. Spitbubble should be here soon."

Brains started up the corridor, and Lint stationed himself in front of the entryway, sitting so that his huge frame took up almost the entire opening. With his back to Birch, he immediately reached into his pocket and took out a pouch. From the pouch, he removed what looked like a large, fuzzy ball. Then, he pushed up his T-shirt and started to poke around in his navel. Birch watched as Lint's hand finally emerged, holding a surprisingly large collection of belly button lint. With his other hand, Lint reached his pinkie into his ear and gave the finger two and a half strong rotations. The finger resurfaced with a thick glob of earwax. More delicately than Birch had seen him do anything else, Lint proceeded to use the earwax to add the new specimens to his ball.

"No-Bone, I need you to go back to the science museum one more time." Brains's voice suddenly came booming out of the very walls.

Birch was startled. The voice was definitely coming from upstairs, but the acoustics of the cavern worked in such a way as to make it sound like a PA system was broadcasting right into his little cell.

"But I already stole the keycard," he heard No-Bone say.

"I know. And good work. But I need you to finish this camera diagram. I'm pretty sure we're covered, but I want to be absolutely positive there won't be any surprises tomorrow."

There was the sound of rustling paper.

Birch glanced quickly over at Lint, who was still lovingly attending to his lint ball. He didn't seem to be at all alarmed by the voices, or how clearly Birch could make out every word.

"You have to go," Snotshot said sarcastically, "because Lint wasn't able to do his only job today correctly. Shocking, I know."

At this, Lint jerked his head up and looked toward the staircase. Birch could see an angry grimace on his face. But, moments later, he shook his head. Almost absentmindedly, he picked up one of the rather large pieces of rock strewn about, and started to do bicep curls with his left arm, while continuing to roll the ball around with his right.

"It won't take long," Brains said.

"Okay, fine. I need to do a little shopping anyway," No-Bone said.

"In case your plan doesn't work, Brains," Snotshot started, "I'm going to think of some ways to distract the guard once we're in."

"My plan will work," Brains said coolly.

"Yeah, sure," Snotshot said. "Still, just in case, I've thought of some good scenarios I can act out if we need to. You know, lost and scared little girl, dumb and confused little girl, that sort of thing. I'm good at improvising."

"Improvising?" No-Bone asked.

"Yes. I used to be in the school plays, you know."

"When were you ever in school enough to rehearse plays?" came No-Bone's amused drawl.

"Shut up!"

Birch heard a loud thud that reverberated down the wall and into his whole back. Snotshot must pack a pretty mean punch.

"Ow! You're crazy!" came No-Bone's muffled reply.

Lint didn't look particularly perturbed. He merely switched the arm doing the bicep curls.

From upstairs, Birch heard approaching footsteps and a different voice say, "I'm back." It was the kid with the curly hair and monkey shirt.

"And I'm leaving," No-Bone said as the sound of diminishing footsteps came through.

"What did you get, Toe Jam?" asked Brains.

There was silence for a bit. "Great. That should be worth a lot," Brains said.

"Toulouse claims it's been in my family for two hundred years," Toe Jam said.

"Way to get back at the 'rents," Snotshot's snarky voice came through.

"Like they'll notice. They haven't noticed anything else yet."

"That's an astounding amount of neglect. You must be proud," Snotshot said.

"Well, anyway, Spitbubble will be happy. He'll probably bring it in to Barnes later," Brains said.

"Talking about me? Behind my back?" came a new voice, this one much deeper than anyone else's. The voice rolled around its consonants like heavy boulders, slowly and with great power.

"Spitbubble . . . ," Brains said quickly. Birch thought he could detect a tiny note of anxiety in his voice. "Look what Toe Jam got today."

Spitbubble waited a few moments before answering, letting the silence crackle with anticipation. "Nice," he finally said. "I'll work on this. Everything set for tomorrow?"

"All set, Spitbubble," came Snotshot's reply.

"Good," the voice thundered.

There was a pause. Finally Brains spoke. "Um, we do have a little . . . situation."

"Situation?"

"Yes, we caught an intruder today."

Oh no, Birch thought. *This is not good. Not good.*

"An intruder in the cavern?" Spitbubble asked.

"No, in the woods," Brains said.

"But we think he may have heard part of tomorrow's plan. That's why *I* suggested we bring him here and let you decide what to do with him," Snotshot interjected.

"I see."

There was another moment of silence.

"Well, take me to him then," came Spitbubble's voice.

Birch heard a large shuffle and then the absolutely terrifying sound of a few pairs of sneakers moving down the long hallway that would eventually lead to his pounding heart.

ENTER SPITBUBBLE

The leading footsteps were slow and deliberate, as if they had all the time in the world. With every one, Birch felt his inner terror meter level up. He clenched his eyes shut, wishing that the peanut butter concoction from that morning had been real and that, instead of being about to meet the supervillain he was sure would destroy him, he was safe in his bed with a severe stomachache. If only adults had told him the truth about why he should never lie, about the terrifying groups of kids that lived in the forest just waiting to kidnap you should you ever put a toe out of line.

Though his eyes were closed, Birch could feel his lids darken as a shadow blocked out the light coming from the stairs. This was it.

There was only one thing Birch could do, and that was

to not cry. Goldenrod wouldn't cry and neither should he—no matter what they did to him.

He peeled open his lids, blinking as he laid eyes on the boy for the first time.

He *was* a boy, although clearly older than the rest of the kids. He was extremely skinny, so much so that even his shadow was only a sliver on the ground of Birch's cell. He was tall, too, and the shadow seemed to creep up the walls to the ceiling. The flashlight behind Birch's head illuminated his face, and Birch could make out messy jet-black hair atop a scrawny face with a pointed nose and patchy stubble. His eyes were as black as his hair.

"Leave us," the deep voice said, seeming to come from somewhere beyond the large Adam's apple jutting out of the boy's bony neck.

Birch saw Lint step away from the door and heard his and the others' footsteps as they climbed back up the stairs.

The boy leaned against the doorway and folded his arms. He smiled at Birch, clearly cherishing his ability to stir up fear.

"So," the boy finally said. "My friends tell me you've been spying."

Birch gulped. He opened his mouth to speak but then, worried that talking would only cause a flood of tears, shut his mouth again and resorted to shaking his head.

"Oh, so you weren't spying?"

Birch shook his head again.

"Then what exactly were you doing in the middle of my forest?" Spitbubble's voice was extremely level. If Birch had just heard it under normal circumstances, he probably would have thought it to be the smooth sounds of a TV announcer, the one that told him batteries weren't included.

"Well?" Spitbubble said again, this time cocking his head and fixating his coal-black glare straight into Birch's eyes.

There was no way around it. Birch was going to have to talk.

"I . . . I wasn't spying. I was just . . . playing?" Birch squeaked, thinking how small and insignificant his voice sounded next to Spitbubble's.

"Playing? And where are your parents?"

"At home."

"And they just let their five-year-old come and *play* in the forest. Completely unsupervised? Don't they know what a dangerous world this is?"

Birch fumbled with the straps on his purple-and-gold backpack. For some reason, this gave him the strength to go on. "Well, they didn't exactly let me. I . . . I snuck out."

"Oh, really?" Spitbubble looked amused now.

Feeling a tiny bit braver, Birch continued, "I'm eight, by the way."

"You're a little scrawny for eight. But I guess you are a bit of a rebel, huh?" Spitbubble smirked.

Birch didn't respond but continued to move his fingers up and around the bumpy backpack straps.

"Okay, Tiny. So what did you hear when you were in the forest?"

"Nothing."

"Nothing?"

Birch shook his head.

"You didn't hear the kids talking about, oh, say, some sort of plan?"

Birch shook his head again.

"Nothing?" Spitbubble asked again.

Birch shook his head a little harder.

"You swear?"

Birch nodded. He was now clenching the plastic ring of his backpack very tightly.

"Swear on your family's lives?"

Birch nodded again, afraid to speak lest he betray his fear.

"Okay, so if you didn't hear anything in the forest, what did you hear here?"

"Nothing," Birch replied.

"You didn't hear a single word of conversation your entire time here?"

"Not since they brought me downstairs." Birch's hand was now purple and white from how hard he was pressing it against the plastic.

"Huh. Well, that's interesting." Spitbubble stopped leaning against the wall and stood up in the doorway, cutting the opening perfectly in half with his straight-line of a body.

"Funny thing. I've never really tested the acoustics in this little room. You think these walls are soundproof?"

Spitbubble rapped his knuckles on the wall beside him.

Birch gave a tiny shrug.

"Only one way to find out. Yo, Toe Jam!" Spitbubble yelled up the staircase.

There was the sound of scurrying feet and Toe Jam yelled back, "Yes, Spitbubble?"

"Why don't you stop hanging on to every word I say and tell the rest to do the same."

"Yes, Spitbubble."

"All of you—go in the main room. And have a conversation."

"A conversation?" came Toe Jam's voice.

"Yes. It's where you talk, and then listen when someone else talks. And then maybe you talk again," Spitbubble's deadpan voice retorted.

"Right. But, um, what should we talk about?"

"I don't care. About your collective dead or deadbeat parents. Whatever. Just talk!"

"Right." There was a larger scurry of footsteps, and Birch could hear the kids assemble again in the front room.

"So, um, what did you do today, Snotshot?" Toe Jam's voice came booming right through to Birch's room.

"What kind of a question is that?" Snotshot asked.

"I don't know, he said to talk!" Toe Jam hissed, even that coming across loud and clear.

Spitbubble had now uncrossed his arms and was running one hand over the stubble on his chin.

"Well, Tiny. Here is lesson number one for you. You can lie to your parents all you want. I couldn't care less. In fact, I recommend it." Spitbubble clasped his hands together and pierced Birch's gaze with his own, this time making his eyes into catlike slits. "But never, *ever* . . . lie . . . to . . . me." His voice was soft and deadly now.

"Brains!" he suddenly boomed, causing Birch to jump.

There was the sound of footsteps again, and Brains appeared at the edge of the doorway. "Yes?" he said.

"Lint will keep guarding him. And if he screws up, you're responsible. Got it?"

"Yes," Brains said.

Spitbubble walked away from the door and out of Birch's sight.

"How long will we be holding him?" Brains asked.

"Until I figure out what I'm going to do," came Spitbubble's smooth reply.

"But what about his parents?"

"You think I'm afraid of some stupid adult? I'm sixteen. You know what that means? It means I'm almost an adult too. And smarter, no doubt, than whatever spawned *that*."

It was the only time Birch heard Spitbubble's voice betray a hint of agitation.

Birch could no longer help it; his tears had a mind of their own and a destination planned—and it was decidedly the cavern floor.

After successfully ducking Toulouse, Goldenrod had taken Meriwether's advice and followed Randy. Randy did not make as much noise walking as Charlie and Jonas had, so Goldenrod had to be extra careful to stay quiet while keeping up.

Randy didn't walk very far, but he was definitely headed to a section of the woods Goldenrod had never seen before. She almost gasped when she first laid eyes on his final destination. It was a gigantic red stone entrance that stood within a circle of forest trees. For a second, Goldenrod thought about how excited she would have been had she discovered this structure on her own. Surely, this was completely unmapped territory! But as soon as she saw Randy go in, her thoughts snapped back to Birch at once.

She wasn't positive he was in there; how could she be? But she knew the chances were pretty high that if one jerk from her school was going somewhere, he would most likely be attracting other jerks right along with him. It was like that old saying about attracting flies with honey—except with jerks. Besides, how likely was it that the great Meriwether Lewis was wrong about where something was, especially if he had been haunting this forest for a couple hundred years? That was a whole lot of prime exploration time.

Almost as if to confirm her suspicions, within moments Drew Henderson and his incredible spine came walking out of the cavern. He did a couple of cartwheels and then disappeared into the forest.

Grateful for all the training she and Charla had done together, Goldenrod decided this would be a good time to apply some of the green and brown makeup from her backpack. She did so in record time, using the tiny mirror attached to the compact's lid. Then, camouflaging herself behind the trees that surrounded the structure, Goldenrod walked the perimeter of the giant slab of stone. It was massive, taking her almost a full two minutes to get around, especially as she was trying to do it so carefully and quietly. The other side of the entrance was tall, smooth rock without a single crevice on its surface.

She was coming around the side with the entrance again when something caught the corner of her eye. This time, she was right to feel her pulse quicken. There, only a few feet away from the stone structure, was a single plant: a small bush with deep blue-green leaves and at least a dozen vivid blue roses sprouting from it. The flowers were practically glowing, almost as if they were plugged into some invisible electrical outlet.

Goldenrod gasped. "Meriwether!" she said in a loud whisper.

There was no answer. She was about to say, "I found it!" when she had to use her own hand to clamp her mouth shut. Striding up to the entrance of the rock was a very tall boy she hadn't seen before. She caught a glimpse of messy black hair and a profile of a long nose and then he too was inside the cavern.

Silently, Goldenrod swore that she would come back to the rosebush later, reclaim Meriwether's lost discovery, and set his spirit free once and for all. But for now, she was going to have to focus on a different heroic mission: rescuing her brother.

Goldenrod waited to see if anyone else would enter or come out of the cavern. No one did. Slowly, she started to make her way back around to the front, all the time listening for any sign of the kids she had seen that morning or, most importantly, for Birch. But there was nothing.

Goldenrod stared at the entrance, not knowing at all what to do. Still, she couldn't allow herself to hesitate for long. Her mind was flooded with how scared Birch must be in the hands of some of her least favorite people.

Still slowly, she started to emerge from behind the trees and walk toward the stone entrance. With every step, she felt braver and more like a true Legendary Adventurer. No one seemed to be coming out, and the forest was filled with the same comforting sounds of birds and rustling leaves she had grown so accustomed to, without the alien sounds of sneakers or snapping twigs disrupting them.

Goldenrod finally reached the entrance. She stopped and poked her head around the corner of it. She was looking into a large red hallway with flashlights taped to the walls. At the end of it, she could see a rough sort of staircase.

It was completely empty, so she stepped in. Quietly making her way across the stone floor, she decided that down those stairs was as good a place to start as any.

It was at the exact moment that she reached the top landing that the tall boy emerged from the darkness of the staircase and almost stepped on Goldenrod's foot.

MORE LIES

The boy looked almost as startled to see Goldenrod as she was to see him, but he was able to hide it quicker.

He grabbed her by the arm. "Who are you?" he asked.

At first, Goldenrod didn't answer. He shook her a little. "I said, who are you?"

He wasn't yelling but he was scary just the same, and there was something unsettlingly familiar about being held in his dark gaze.

"Dahlia," Goldenrod muttered.

"Dahlia what?"

"Meriwether," Goldenrod answered without hesitation, again silently thankful for all those times she had had Charla play Formidable Foe.

"What are you doing here, Ms. *Meriwether*?" the boy sneered, stretching out her fake last name.

"I was taking a walk."

"Taking a walk? Your parents let you just come into the woods all by yourself? With green makeup on?"

"Yes, they do."

The boy still had Goldenrod by the arm. She pulled herself slightly to get out of his grasp. "If you'll excuse me," she said.

The boy grabbed her arm tighter. "Nope, don't think I will."

Just then, Goldenrod heard footsteps behind the boy, and from the staircase emerged the figure of Jonas. He looked just as surprised to see her as the older boy had a minute earlier. Only he, of course, knew exactly who she was.

"Mold-and-rot!" he exclaimed.

"Mold-and-rot?" the older boy asked.

"That's Goldenrod Moram, Spitbubble. The little boy is her brother," Jonas said. "Wait, why do you look like a tree?"

Well, if nothing else she had at least done a decent job with the makeup.

The older boy turned back to Goldenrod, his gaze darker than ever. "So, you thought you'd lie to me?" he asked softly.

"Not really a lie. I could've been named Dahlia," Goldenrod muttered.

"How did you find us?" he asked.

Goldenrod remained silent, her brain reeling as to how to get herself and Birch out of all this.

"Answer me." It appeared as if the older boy—who apparently was the same Spitbubble she had heard mention of earlier—had no intention of letting go of Goldenrod's arm.

"You're not going to answer me?" he said, tightening his grasp on her wrist.

Goldenrod stared defiantly into Spitbubble's eyes. Not a word escaped her lips.

"Admirable." The boy sounded like he was almost laughing as he turned to Jonas. "Drag her brother up here. Let's see if she keeps her silence as easily if it's his arm."

"No!" Goldenrod blurted.

Spitbubble turned to her and spoke slowly and calmly, "Just one more chance, then. How did you find us?"

Somehow, Goldenrod didn't think the boy would be terribly understanding about a story involving a ghost with a finely tuned sense of direction, one actually named Meriwether at that. So she skipped that part and came up with, "I followed Randy."

There was a glint of anger in the boy's eyes before they darkened again. He slackened his hold on Goldenrod's arm and yelled, "Toe Jam!" into the cavern.

Within a few seconds, there were more scuffling footsteps, and the staircase produced the dirty, ruffled frame of Randy.

"Yes, Spitbubble?"

So Randy is . . . Toe Jam? Goldenrod thought.

"This girl here tells us that she followed you all the way to Headquarters."

Toe Jam's jaw dropped as he saw Goldenrod. "Mold-and-rot . . . ," his voice trailed.

"Explain yourself," Spitbubble said.

"I . . . I don't know how she got here," Toe Jam said.

"Where were you when you saw him?" Spitbubble asked Goldenrod.

"Due west," Goldenrod grumbled.

"Are you trying to be funny?" Spitbubble asked.

"No. If I was, I wouldn't be doing a very good job."

"Shut up and answer the question. I don't need any extra words out of you," Spitbubble said.

"I was answering your question. I was due west." Goldenrod looked at the blank faces staring at her and sighed, pointing to where she had come from. "Over there, by a bunch of bushes with red berries."

Spitbubble rounded on Toe Jam. "Well?"

"I don't know . . . maybe she means where I was meeting Toulouse," he said.

"Toe Jam, I believe this is the second time I've warned you about bringing your *butler* into these woods." He exaggerated the word *butler* in the same slow, dangerous way he had exaggerated *Meriwether*.

"How else am I supposed to get the stuff from him?" Toe Jam muttered.

"Oh, I don't know. By going to the house where you live and he works and where no one will suspect you hanging around. The fact that you actually have a house you can go to and get that junk from is the only use I have for you." Spitbubble didn't blink once, penetrating Toe Jam with his glare. "And, if you can't even do that right, well . . ."

"That junk seems to pay for a lot of things," Toe Jam mumbled.

"It pays for the privilege of letting you hang out with us. You don't want to do it anymore, no problem. The exit is that way . . . *due west*," Spitbubble pointed.

That shut Toe Jam up. For a minute, Spitbubble continued to glare at him. And then he turned away as if nothing had happened. He handed Goldenrod's arm to Jonas.

"Take her down and keep her with her brother, Brains. Until I figure out how to clean up your mess."

Birch had stopped crying, but he couldn't stop sniffling. He needed to figure out how to get himself out of there.

Maybe he could tackle—SNIFF—Lint with one of those video-game moves he had practiced—SNIFF—all summer. Then he'd run upstairs screaming an ear-shattering battle cry, take down the rest of the kids in one truly spectacular roundhouse kick, and run back home and into his bed right before his mother—SNIFF—would be coming in with a hot bowl of soup.

As he was visualizing this awesome feat, he heard more footsteps on the stairs.

"We got another one," he heard Brains say.

Lint looked up. "What's *she* doing here?"

"Guard her, Lint. This is no joke. Spitbubble's in a foul mood."

And then Birch saw her—she was being led into the room by Brains. Birch's face broke into a wide grin.

Goldenrod loosened herself from Brains's grasp and hurried over to him. Birch immediately threw himself at her, holding on to her in a tight hug.

Goldenrod patted him on the head. Birch was so happy and relieved to see her that it was a few moments before he began to realize that if Goldenrod were in here—who on earth was out there to rescue him?

THE LAB

So you know that girl, right, Brains? You know her family?" Spitbubble said as Brains came back up the stairs. He was leaning against the cavern wall, arms folded in front of his thin chest.

"Yeah . . . ," Brains trailed off.

"Good. Think of a way of scaring her and that little brat into never breathing a word of this to anyone. I expect you to make good on your nickname." Spitbubble straightened himself out. "And make sure everything is set for tomorrow," he said casually as he strolled out of the cavern.

Easy for him to say, Brains thought to himself about a half hour later as he kicked a pebble moodily and walked into the bright sunshine. He was always the one that was coming up with the plans. *Then again, who else would do it?* he thought as he looked to the clearing by the side of the cavern and saw No-Bone, Toe Jam, and Snotshot arguing while they were trying to make up teams for a game of tug-of-war. Toe Jam had created a nice mud pit with the help of the hose that Brains had hooked up a few weeks ago and they were using an old, frayed rope that one of them had picked up from somewhere. It was getting hard to keep track of who was contributing what to their inventory.

Toe Jam spotted him as he walked toward them.

"You're on my team, Brains."

Brains shook his head. "I can't. I have work to do for Spitbubble."

"In your super secret lab, I bet," Snotshot snorted.

"It's not super secret. It's just super secret to you because you don't understand what I'm doing," Brains said coolly.

"Brains, no one understands what you're doing. Albert Einstein would probably have a hard time," Snotshot said.

Brains smirked smugly.

"Although," Snotshot continued, "perhaps Thomas Edison might have a clue."

Brains glared at her. She knew how he felt about that backstabber Edison.

"Without me—" he started.

"Yes, yes, we know," No-Bone said, as he grabbed hold of one end of the rope. "There would never be a plan, and we'd all be doomed to go back to our homes."

"And don't you forget it," Brains said.

"How could we? You won't let us," No-Bone said.

"Brains, are you going to play or not?" Toe Jam asked.

"Not," Brains said.

"Okay, fine. Then I'll be on Snotshot's team," Toe Jam said, a little too eagerly.

"Dude, no way," No-Bone said. "This is how we always team up. How else are we going to keep ultimate score?"

"But this isn't fair!" Toe Jam said. "Lint's not here to be on my team. Unless he can come out—" Toe Jam looked hopefully at Brains.

"Absolutely not," Brains said. "Lint's on guard, and he's staying there."

"Fine," Toe Jam said. "New teams, then."

"You can't always be on the winning side, Toe Jam," No-Bone said. "It'll be good for you to learn how to be a gracious loser." He smirked.

"Who are you calling a loser?" Toe Jam said and then, after a pause, "Seriously though, you're both older and bigger than me. How is this fair?"

"Oh, fine," Snotshot butted in. "Stop your whining. I'll be on a side by myself."

Brains took one last glance at Toe Jam's defeated face. He could almost see the wheels turning in his head, trying to think of a clever reason to be on Snotshot's team instead.

Brains rolled his eyes as he turned around.

"Wait," No-Bone called, and ran up to give him the

crumpled piece of grid paper. "Here, I finished the camera diagram."

"Great. We're all set," Brains said.

While No-Bone returned to his rowdy game of tug-of-war, Brains walked deeper into the woods. He needed to go to a place with no distractions.

Soon, the other kids' voices were replaced with the sound of a running stream. As soon as he heard the water, he let himself do what he never allowed himself to in front of the others—worry. So much of what everyone had done hinged on his plans and thoughts. What if something were to go wrong? What if they couldn't get the right equipment tomorrow or, worse, what if he'd miscalculated something and the generator wouldn't work at all?

And now, on top of everything else, he had to find a way to scare the Morams. As Brains passed by all the lush forest greenery, he was instantly reminded of the most vivid thing he knew about them: that they lived in a nice house with sweet parents and a pretty extraordinary garden.

He had played in that garden a lot way back in kindergarten, when the foster home he was staying at was only a block away from the Morams' house. He remembered how he and Goldenrod had dug holes for tulip bulbs while her mother had brought them out peach iced tea and fruit snacks. Every now and again, when he had happened to pass by the Morams' house in the springtime, he had seen those tulips, now grown purple, red, and yellow, and he'd been reminded of that happy and simple summer.

But that was a long time and many foster homes ago. *This is my home now*, he thought, as he stepped into a small stone cave situated right by the stream.

Unlike the lair, this cave consisted of only one longish room. Most of it was taken up by a large wooden table on top of which lay all sorts of beakers, Bunsen burners, wires, plugs, circuit boards, a microscope, a telescope, and other various scientific instruments. Most of the equipment came as a result of meshing together a few different chemistry sets. Some of the supplies No-Bone had graciously nicked from the middle school laboratory before school let out. And some, like the telescope and a lot of the electric wires, Spitbubble had actually allotted some money to because he believed in their importance.

In a lot of ways, the lab was the greatest part of being a member of the Gross-Out Gang. Obviously, Brains was aware that he was smart, but it was one of the first times he felt that someone else really appreciated it. None of his foster parents had ever stuck around long enough to really know that about him: troublemaker, yes, but brilliant troublemaker, not so much. Even though, really, how was a scientist supposed to come up with new theories and inventions if he didn't accidentally blow up a basement or two?

"Right?" Brains said directly to the poster that was

taped above his workstation. A man with gelled black hair, a mustache, and a slight smile looked back at him. His hero, Nikola Tesla.

Tesla was a pioneer in electricity and radio. He invented the Tesla coil, capable of shooting one million volts of electricity into the air, which he loved to use during demonstrations simply to keep his audience on their toes. He would amaze and confound them by lighting bulbs that were plugged into nowhere. He helped invent robots and remote controls. And he was a bit of a mad scientist. In a word, he was the very definition of awesome.

Oh, and he'd had a pretty serious rivalry going on with Thomas Edison. Brains was totally on Tesla's side, of course.

The thing was, if Tesla could come up with all those ideas in the late nineteenth century, surely Brains could solve the Gross-Out Gang's problems with just a little bit of help from twenty-first century equipment.

Brains closed his eyes and listened for the faint sound of gurgling. That gurgling came from the underground hot springs that started below the lab and ran all the way to the giant lair. And that gurgling was the key to Brains's plan to bring heat and electricity to the lair and to make the forest a permanent home for all of them.

He allowed himself a small smile.

A short while later, Brains was putting on a disguise in the form of a navy baseball cap attached to a blond mullet—probably a donation from Snotshot's old theater department. He put his new, carefully prepared brown box underneath one arm, gave a final nod to Tesla, and set out to, as Spitbubble had said, make good on his nickname.

GOLDENROD'S FAN BASE

Goldenrod and Birch had been sitting side by side against the cavern wall for only a few seconds when Goldenrod had to ask, "How did you get here?" She whispered it to him, keeping an eye on Lint's massive back, which was blocking their exit.

Birch looked guilty. "I followed you," he finally whispered back.

"Why?"

"I dunno. I was bored. Whatever you were doing seemed like more fun than being at home . . . What *were* you doing, anyway?"

Goldenrod shrugged. Considering all that had happened, it now seemed silly to keep her mapmaking such a big, dark secret. "Oh, I was just drawing a map," she finally said.

"A map?"

"Yeah, a really detailed map of all of Pilmilton. That's why I was exploring the woods."

"Is that why you're all green and brown and stuff?"

"Well, I was trying to blend in so they wouldn't see me—" Goldenrod started.

"Cool!" Birch's blotchy face suddenly brightened, and Goldenrod had to smile. If only everyone else in the world was as big a fan of hers as he was. For a moment, she thought about telling Birch all about Meriwether too. But when she looked into his eyes and saw dark pools of worry, she reconsidered. It seemed like Birch might have already had enough frights for one day and ghost stories were probably not going to help.

"How did you land in the middle of that clearing?" Goldenrod whispered instead.

"I lost you for a minute when you started running. And then I was just following the sound of your footsteps, and before I knew it—"

"Jonas and Charlie," Goldenrod interjected.

"They call themselves Brains and Lint here," Birch whispered. "And the girl is Snotshot. And then there's No-Bone and Toe Jam." Birch counted off on his fingers. "And, of course, Spitbubble."

Goldenrod was impressed. "Looks like you've picked up a lot."

"Yeah, well, I also happened to hear all about their plan

to break into the museum tomorrow. Which is probably why they're not going to let us go." Birch looked sad again.

Goldenrod had gathered as much too, though she still couldn't figure out what on earth they could want from the science museum. "Well, we're here together now," she said brightly to Birch. "Like Dad always says, two Morams are better than one!"

Birch gave a weak smile. He was silent for a minute before speaking again. "I did something kinda bad to get here," he finally said.

"What do you mean?"

"Mom—she thinks I'm sick and in bed. She has to know by now that I'm gone. She'll be so upset . . ." Birch's voice trailed off.

Goldenrod put her arm around his shoulder and whispered even more softly, close in his ear, "We'll find a way out of here. We have to."

Mrs. Moram had spent a very satisfying morning in her garden, pruning and weeding. Her dahlias were coming along exceptionally well this summer, a particularly bright, purple one causing her an immense amount of cheer. She'd have to take a picture and send it in to the Dahlia Society. It definitely had a shot of ending up in next month's newsletter.

She'd hardly noticed the time go by as she worked in

the sun. It had been cool and breezy for July, one of those perfect gardening days, and she had so enjoyed her time outside that she all but forgot her other responsibilities.

It was only when she heard Mr. Chen, one of her neighbors, call in his son for lunch that she realized she was hungry. And goodness, Birch must be too.

Mrs. Moram first went into the kitchen and rummaged around in a cabinet. She found a can of chicken noodle soup in the very back. She popped it open and set about heating it up which, unlike Mr. Moram and his obsession with food creation, was about as complicated as her cooking skills ever got. While the soup was bubbling, she poured a glass of orange juice and toasted a piece of bread in the special "smiley-face" setting of their toaster. She smeared the toast with some strawberry jam, ladled the soup into Birch's favorite bowl, and set up the whole meal on a little tray. Then she took out a small, skinny vase and filled it with a few of the budding goldenrods that she had plucked that morning.

She smiled as she artfully arranged the tall, bright yellow stalks. Mrs. Moram knew that goldenrods were an odd choice of favorite flower for a gardener. They weren't necessarily the prettiest and, in fact, were often mistaken for weeds. But she found them beautiful and resilient. She loved their bold, unapologetic yellow color. She loved that they were wildflowers, not easily killed or intimidated like a lot of the other more traditionally cultivated species. They were strong instead of delicate, and she thought that every garden should have a good mixture of both.

When the whole thing looked just right, Mrs. Moram took the tray and set off upstairs.

She entered Birch's quiet room. He was lying very still on his bed. *He must be really sick*, she thought to herself, feeling sorry for her poor son.

She gently put the tray down on his bedside table and went to rearrange the covers around him.

BUZZ!!!

It was their exceptionally loud doorbell. Mrs. Moram jumped and, in doing so, moved the covers a little with her hand, causing her to think that Birch had stirred.

"Seed of the Month Club Delivery," she heard a loud and cheerful voice calling.

"Oh, I'm sorry to wake you, sweetie. Let me go get that, and I'll come check on you in a bit, okay? Have some soup," she said, as she hurried excitedly out of Birch's room and toward the front door.

16

A DISHONEST LIVING

Spitbubble was proud of his height; it allowed him to look rather menacing when he walked, as he placed one firm marchlike step in front of the other. It also helped that he kept his fists balled up at all times, as if ready for a brawl with anyone in his warpath. But he knew that his strongest weapon was his black glare, the way it could, and had, stopped many people in the middle of a conversation, made them falter, made them show weakness.

He was using this glare now as he stared across a glass counter to a leather-faced man with a stringy ponytail hanging morosely from his otherwise bald head. The man was examining Toe Jam's gold coin minutely.

"Looks dirty," he finally grunted.

"That's because it's old. Antique. Check out the date." Spitbubble pointed to the ancient date inscribed on the coin's surface.

"Humph," the man, called Barnes, said.

They were standing inside Barnes's Barn, Pilmilton's tiny pawnshop that was filled to the brim with useless junk that people had cast off through the years. The case Barnes and Spitbubble were leaning over was filled with probably at least fifty items in and of itself: clocks that had no hands, tarnished earrings with no mate, an object that might have either been a medieval torture device or a really dirty spork.

Spitbubble, however, knew that this junk wasn't how Barnes really made his living. The store mostly served as a front for the kinds of things that Barnes really collected and sold to handpicked clientele. Things like famously misplaced paintings and the rare and valuable coin he was now turning over in his hands.

"I'll give you seventy-five bucks," Barnes finally said.

"That's not what this is worth," Spitbubble said calmly.

"If you can find someone else who's willing to pay more, I'll gladly consider a counteroffer," Barnes sneered. Being the only pawnshop owner in town had its advantages, especially if you also happened to be okay with more than a little dishonesty.

Spitbubble thought for a minute, took in a deep breath, and then quick as a flash snatched the coin out of Barnes's hand and returned it to his pocket. "All right. No biggie. See you later, then."

He barely got a glimpse of Barnes's utterly startled face as he calmly turned on his heels and strode the two steps it took to reach the front door. He had just pushed it open when he heard, "Wait."

He turned around calmly and stared at the man, who was now stretching his cracked lips into something that might be considered a smile in a creepy, horror-movie-bellhop sort of way. "I can see I'm dealing with a pro here," Barnes said.

"I don't have time for your hot air," Spitbubble said breezily. "We both know that I have a one-of-a-kind and valuable item."

"And we both know it wasn't exactly left to you by your dear, dead aunt Gertrude," Barnes grumbled.

They glared at each other for a moment. "Three hundred," Barnes finally said.

"Five hundred," Spitbubble said.

"Three-fifty is my final offer," Barnes said. "I could have you arrested, you know."

"Ditto," Spitbubble said coolly. He used his black glare one more time with his hand still on the shop door.

"Fine! Four hundred. But that is absolutely it, you sniveling brat."

❋

Spitbubble smiled as he marched into the most perfect-looking suburban block any television show creator could have imagined. The whole street was lined with big, leafy maple trees, and each house was a slightly different color combination than the next. One was pink with a gray roof. The next, green with a black roof. The next, yellow with a blue roof. And so on. Each different, but the same.

With his infamous glare, Spitbubble zoned in on one particular house, the gray one with the black roof, and strode up to it. He opened the gate of the house's white picket fence, marched up the driveway, and banged a fist on the front door, causing it to swing open easily. He strode into the quiet, pristine house as if he owned the place, smirking a little at the mahogany furniture, matching beige sofa set, and, most especially, ginormous framed black-and-white photo that hung over the fireplace. It was of a young dark-haired boy in a patterned sweater, grinning a missing-toothed grin, and posing with one hand under his chin.

"Stannie, is that you?" came a low female voice from some other part of the house.

"Yeah, Ma," Spitbubble said. He strode through the front hallway and down a few steps into the den, which was filled with more matching furniture and a fake green Persian rug with an intricately hideous pattern on its surface. He sat down on a sunken violet couch and took out a large wad of cash from the pocket that had once housed the heavy, gold coin. The cash was a lot less shiny, but a lot more attractive to Spitbubble's eye.

At that moment a tall, dark-haired woman walked into the den. She was wearing a beige short-sleeved blouse and a shapeless brown skirt: *teacher clothes*, Spitbubble thought, even though it was still summer vacation and she wouldn't be back in the classroom for a few weeks yet.

"How was your day, Stannie?" she asked her son.

"Good, Ma," he said as he counted out the money one more time to make sure that Barnes hadn't shortchanged him.

The woman walked over and squinted at what he was doing. "Another good garage sale find?"

"Mmm-hmmm."

The woman chuckled as she patted Spitbubble on the head. "Oh, Stan. You have such a head for business. Lord knows how you spot these things. Who are all these stupid people selling their valuables in garage sales left and right?!"

"Well, you know what they say, Ma. One man's junk is another man's treasure," Spitbubble answered.

The woman giggled and beamed at her son. "They sure do. You're going to save yourself so much money for college, Stannie."

"Mmmm." Spitbubble smiled back, all the while staring at the purple bags under his mother's eyes and inwardly swearing that he'd never fall to the same fate as her, looking old and tired while trying to earn an honest living. An honest living was for chumps and lame-os; Barnes knew that and so did he. Instead, Spitbubble was going to make enough money to be able to skip college and do whatever he wanted. He was determined to make adulthood *fun*.

All he had to do was get Brains to rig up the lair for heat and electricity, and then those hot springs would create the perfect natural spa for people like his mother. Tired, stressed-out adults who would pay a lot of money for a little bit of relaxation. *A close-by getaway for when you don't have time to get away.* Or something like that. He'd have to work on the slogan. Oh, and getting those kids out of the forest by the time he was ready to open the spa. Though it shouldn't be too hard to anonymously tip off the cops about a bunch of orphaned and runaway kids hiding out in the forest.

"What do you want for dinner? Is meatloaf okay?" his mother asked, bringing him back—for the moment—to his present-day situation.

"Yum," Stan Barbroff said.

TWO MORAMS ARE BETTER THAN ONE

*S*weet, thought Lint to himself as he threw his lint ball on the floor and watched it bounce high. This was his sixty-fourth lint creation and the best of them all. Building the lint around a rubber ball had been a stroke of genius and, most importantly, he had come up with the idea completely on his own. Lint wasn't stupid, but he knew enough to know that the rest of the kids thought he *was* pretty stupid. His father and his six brothers and sisters wouldn't argue against it either—that is, if they were to ever bother thinking about him at all. He had now slept in the cavern, away from home, for over a whole week straight and no one had come looking for him. For the tiniest, most fleeting second, he allowed himself to wonder, if his mother had been around, whether she would have realized he was missing. But then he bounced the lint ball particularly high and let his pride in his own handiwork drive that thought right out.

Something silver came whirring at Lint's ball just then and knocked it out of its perfect bounce trail. Lint looked up to see two more silver things flying toward him. He ducked just in time.

"Whoops," No-Bone yelled from the top of the staircase.

Lint grunted and looked down to see what had nearly blinded him. It was three chocolate protein bars. His favorite kind, actually. He forgot about the near blindness and picked them up.

"Those are for the Morams," No-Bone yelled back.

"Why?"

"Because Brains said we can't let them starve, man. Just give it to them, okay?"

Lint stared down at the protein bars, eyebrows furrowed. They were his contribution to the group's food supply.

"We're leaving for a little while," No-Bone continued. "Need privacy to talk through some things. Brains said be careful with the prisoners."

Lint smirked as he pointed behind him. "Them? What're they gonna do, tremble to death?" He chuckled at his own cleverness.

"Yeah, yeah. Just watch 'em, okay?" No-Bone disappeared from the top of the stairs, and Lint could hear him and the others leaving the cavern.

He stared down at the three bars. He immediately pock-
eted one, and was about to turn around to give his prisoners
the other two. But then he came to his senses. Honestly, the
two of them probably couldn't even finish one whole bar
between them, let alone two. No point in wasting perfectly
good food that had personally cost him a decent amount of
effort.

He tore one open and took an enormous bite that nearly
finished off the entire thing. With the foil-wrapped stub in
his hand, he turned around to give Mold-and-rot and her
brother the other bar that he had so generously spared for
them.

Except that when he turned around, there was no Mold-
and-rot and her brother—there was just the girl, asleep in an
exhausted pile in the middle of the room, her head resting on
the two backpacks that were against a small ledge in one
of the walls.

"What the . . . ," Lint started. Where was the boy?

"Hey! Hey!" he started to shout, waving the sticky chocolate stub around frantically.

Goldenrod stirred and suddenly woke with a start.

"Where is he?" Lint shouted.

Goldenrod got up, looking momentarily confused at the
sight of Lint.

"Where's the shrimp?" Lint was now flailing his arms
around so much that the remaining bit of protein bar finally
flew out of his hand. He didn't even notice.

Suddenly seeming to remember, Goldenrod gave a sharp intake of breath. "Birch . . ." She started to look around frantically. "Where's Birch? What did you do to my brother?" She stared accusingly at Lint.

"I didn't do anything . . ."

"Then where is he? Did he escape?"

"Escape?" Lint's face fell. He stood there quite motionless for a second, watching the wasted chocolate piece melting on the cavern floor. "Escape?" he said again, before suddenly snapping out of it and springing to action. "Oh my God. I have to tell the others. They'll kill me. You stay here!" He pointed menacingly at Goldenrod.

And with that, Lint had turned around and was climbing the steps two by two.

As soon as Lint had his back to them, Birch finally allowed himself to breathe. He was pretty small, but even he had to suck in his tiny stomach to be able to crouch behind the ledge and be completely invisible, with the extra help of both his and Goldenrod's backpacks.

Just that one breath was all he let himself have before bursting out from behind the ledge. He tried very hard to hoist Goldenrod's now extremely heavy backpack, but his little shoulders couldn't handle it. Goldenrod immediately ran over to help him—it took all her strength to lift it as well.

They had no time to waste. Birch put his now lightened backpack over one shoulder, and the two of them bounded out of their prison and up the stairs in a flash.

They saw Lint heading toward the exit and they leaped after him.

The Morams moved so lightly that, even with the one heavy backpack and the speed they were going, Lint didn't hear them until they were almost right behind him, just as he was getting ready to yell out for help. He immediately turned around and was promptly hit in the gut with what looked, and probably felt, like a giant green bowling ball.

Goldenrod had used all of her strength to swing the backpack into Lint, and the effect was exactly as intended. He was completely winded and fell clear off his feet.

But that wasn't all. Per their plan, Birch already had the roll of duct tape ready to go. He pulled off a long piece and quickly wrapped it around Lint's wrists. Then he moved on to his ankles.

Lint was still wheezing and out of breath, but his voice was coming back to him. "Hey . . . ," he started to roar, followed by a very muffled "*phmmmmmmmmm.*"

Birch looked up from taping Lint's ankles to see that Goldenrod had stuffed her yellow baby sock into Lint's orange-stained mouth. The looks of pure revolt on both Lint's and Goldenrod's faces were almost identical.

Birch knew she had a thing for that sock, but this was no time to get sentimental. He grabbed Goldenrod's hand, and together they bolted right past the silent and horizontal Lint. Not even daring to look back, they tore away from the cavern.

THE LOST DISCOVERY

Goldenrod and Birch ran pell-mell away from the cavern. They were heading due west—back through the only route Goldenrod was sure would lead them out, because she had mapped it.

The thought of her map caused a small ache in her side that had nothing to do with how fast she was running. In order to get her backpack as heavy as it had been, they had filled it with all of the biggest objects they had—which, aside from a few rocks they found on the cavern floor, also included Goldenrod's notebooks and sketches that she had worked on all summer. She doubted very highly that someone like Lint would ever appreciate all the work that had gone into making them . . . and now Charla would never get to see them either.

All they had taken with them was Goldenrod's compass, the roll of duct tape, the garden shears, and one specimen jar.

As Goldenrod caught a glimpse of bright blue from the corner of her eye, she remembered why she had thought to stuff those last two items into Birch's backpack.

"Wait!" she called out.

Birch looked back at her in alarm but didn't stop running.

"I have to . . . cut three of those roses," Goldenrod panted, pointing at the blue rosebush.

"What?! Why?" Birch looked at her, his big blue eyes widening.

"Because," Goldenrod paused, "they're undiscovered flora."

Now Birch was looking at her as if she had not only completely lost her mind, but that it was dancing a jig on top of her head. "We have to get out of here," he said slightly maniacally.

"I know. We will," Goldenrod said as she unzipped Birch's backpack and took out the jar and shears. "This will only take a minute. Just stay right here." Goldenrod motioned to the tree line they were standing in before quickly making her way back across the clearing to the rosebush.

She could almost feel Birch's exasperated stare at her back. Maybe someday she could explain it to him, but now was not the time. For now, she had to do what she had promised—to the old lady, to Meriwether, and, most importantly, to herself when this summer had started.

She kneeled down in front of the rosebush. The old lady had been right about one thing: it smelled of stars and warmth and beach breezes; it smelled just like a summer night. Goldenrod almost felt a little dizzy with its unworldly scent.

She had to focus, though. She reached her hand to get a good hold on one of the stems. Almost as soon as she did, she pulled it back with a yelp. A small but growing drop of blood had appeared on her finger. Goldenrod looked closer at where she had touched the stem and could now make out the tiny, almost imperceptible, but razor-sharp thorns that seemed to cover just about the entire thing. Gently, she reached for the petals of the flower instead, trying to get a grip on them so she could cut the plant. Before she had a chance to snip, though, the most extraordinary thing happened.

One second, her finger was sore and bleeding some-what heavily. And the next, she could see the blood draw its way back in and the wound close up. Goldenrod stared in utter astonishment. Her finger didn't have a scratch on it.

What it did have though, a second later, was a large green glob that had arced its way through the sky and landed right on top of her finger. Goldenrod looked up just in time to see Snotshot running toward her from only about ten feet away.

"Run!" she yelled to Birch, as she grabbed her jar and shears and started to sprint after him through the trees.

They had a decent head start, but Snotshot was still hard on their heels. Birds flew with startled cries, and leaves and twigs snapped away in their paths as they tried to make their escape.

When Goldenrod allowed herself one peek behind to see just how far away their pursuer was, she was startled to instead be staring at a see-through maroon coat.

"Meriwether!" she yelled, still continuing to run. Meriwether didn't seem to have a problem gliding beside and matching her speed, though he looked just as dignified and unruffled as ever.

Out of the corner of her eye, Goldenrod could see that Snotshot was gaining on them. "Why don't you do something?" she said in exasperation to the ghost.

"Like what?" Meriwether asked.

"I don't know. You're a ghost! Go scare her," Goldenrod said.

"Oh," Meriwether said. "That *is* a good idea. Unfortunately, I'm not that kind of ghost. You're the only one who can see me."

"What? Why?"

"Because you're the only one on the quest to find my lost discovery," Meriwether said.

"Seriously?" The breaking twig sounds from behind Goldenrod seemed to be getting closer and closer. "But you've discovered loads of other things," she said. "What could possibly be so special about this one anyway?"

"It saved my life," he said simply. Goldenrod could see him motion to his leg, the one with the limp. "And I have no doubt that it can save countless others too."

Of course! The limp must have come from that time

when Meriwether had been mistakenly shot by one of his own crew members. And hadn't Goldenrod just seen with her own eyes what the rose could do with an injury?

Goldenrod had become so absorbed in these thoughts that she hadn't noticed Birch slowing down considerably. Even though he had started out pretty far ahead, he was right beside her when he looked at her fearfully and asked, "Who are you talking to, Gol—" His question ended in a scream as he was jerked back.

Goldenrod looked over her shoulder to see that Snotshot was holding on to his backpack and, a moment later, his arm.

Goldenrod stopped running immediately. "Let him go!" she yelled.

"Yeah, right," Snotshot said, not sounding nearly as out of breath as Goldenrod felt. "I guess I shouldn't be surprised that big moron let you guys escape."

Birch had started to whimper, and Goldenrod stared at him helplessly.

"So what's the deal, girlie?" Snotshot asked. "Are you going to come quietly or are you going to just let me take your brother back with me?"

PLAN B

Don't leave me alone with them!" Birch yelled.

Of course, she couldn't do that. But she couldn't very well just merrily let both of them get kidnapped again either. What kind of Legendary Adventurer would go along with that?

"What do you want?" she finally asked Snotshot. There was really nothing else to do but be straightforward at this point.

"You're not very bright, are you? Didn't I just say you have to come back to the cave with me?" Snotshot asked slowly, as if speaking to a particularly stupid puppy.

So never mind. Being straightforward didn't seem to be the correct option with someone like Snotshot. Goldenrod was going to have to answer her own question. *Think*, she willed herself and then asked, *What does Spitbubble's crew actually want?* "Money!" she suddenly blurted out. "You want money, don't you?" she said as she thought about what she knew of Toe Jam's coin.

"Sure. Do you have some? I've got no problem unloading it off of you as soon as we get you locked away, safe and sound," Snotshot said.

"No. I know a way you can make some money."

"By holding you for ransom?" Snotshot retorted.

Goldenrod hesitated one moment longer. She didn't particularly like what she was about to do, but she couldn't see any other way out of this mess. "There's this plant," she finally said. "It's undiscovered flora . . . ," she trailed off.

"What are you talking about?" Snotshot asked.

"What are you doing?" a voice asked from beside her. She turned around to see that Meriwether was still standing there. She had almost forgotten about him.

"You want your plant to get discovered, don't you?" she asked wearily.

"Not by them!" he said emphatically. His face had finally slipped from its quiet, dignified mask and was looking rather panicked.

"Well, I need to rescue my little brother!" Goldenrod said, irritated. "And unless you have a better idea, this is the only way I can think of." Honestly, between not being able to scare anybody off and not being terribly useful helping them out from the clutches of Spitbubble's crew, the ghost was starting to get on Goldenrod's nerves—even if he *was* the spirit of her all-time hero.

Meriwether was silent and Goldenrod turned back around in time to see Snotshot ask Birch incredulously, "Is she talking to herself?"

Birch gave a shrug but looked considerably more nervous than before.

"Look." Goldenrod decided to start over again. "It's an undiscovered flower, and it's very rare. It has special properties." She glanced down at her finger, the one that she had cut on the thorn. "Healing properties, I think."

She heard a very small pop beside her and knew that Meriwether had vanished. She was a little sorry to have offended him, and she was very sorry not to be able to complete her mission and claim the discovery for herself, but what choice did she have? At the end of the day, Birch just mattered more.

"So I'm pretty sure it's worth a lot of money," Goldenrod concluded. "And I can tell you where it is, if you just let both of us go."

Snotshot and Birch both stared at Goldenrod. Her brother looked confused and still quite scared. His captor looked as if she was thinking—which was at least a good sign that she was considering the offer.

"And what if you're lying?" she finally asked Goldenrod. "What then?"

"If I'm lying, I really have no doubt you'll find a way to hunt both of us down," Goldenrod said wisely.

"You bet I will," Snotshot snarled, looking pretty pleased with this assessment of herself.

Goldenrod nodded. "And that's why I'm not lying. The flower in question is also close by, so just in case it's not exactly where I say it is, you could probably chase us down anyway."

The girl considered a moment more. "Fine. It's a deal, but—"

"But I also need to know that you'll actually let us go," Goldenrod said firmly. "I need to trust you."

Snotshot scowled a little, but then gave one curt nod. "I'll keep my word."

Goldenrod had nothing to go on but her instincts, but just then, she chose to believe the dirty, older girl. She held out the jar and the gardening shears in front of her. "Let Birch go, and I'll give these to you and tell you exactly where it is."

Snotshot let go of Birch's arm, and he immediately ran over to Goldenrod's side. Goldenrod took the few steps to where Snotshot was and handed her the jar and shears. She then told her exactly where to find the blue rosebush.

"You can't miss it," Goldenrod said. "It's bright, bright blue, and if you smell it, it won't smell like any flower you've ever smelled before. But you have to get it today. It only blooms for three days every fifty years, and today is the last day. When you cut off the flowers, you'll need to seal them in the jar. They'll remain in bloom for one week if you make sure the lid's airtight."

Despite everything, Snotshot at least looked like she was paying attention. If nothing else, maybe the flower would still find its way into the next edition of *The Encyclopedia of North American Flora and Fauna*. Though it didn't make Goldenrod too happy to think of Snotshot's sneering picture next to it.

"When you have it," Goldenrod continued anyway, "take it to a botanist or scientist, okay? They'll know what to do with it." For a moment, she considered warning her about the razor-sharp thorns, but then decided she didn't particularly owe the older girl all of her information. "Just be careful with it," she said. "It's very valuable."

"A flower, huh?" Snotshot asked.

"Yes," Goldenrod said.

"Fine," Snotshot said. "And you won't tell anybody about anything you saw or heard here. Especially this . . . it never happened. Or I will find out, and I will come get you."

Birch looked terrified, but Goldenrod just gave a short nod. Then she grabbed his hand and, without looking back once, they ran.

A BONE TO PICK

Birch ran with wild, almost joyous abandon. Finally, finally they were on their way back home.

He couldn't quite believe how perfectly Goldenrod had engineered their escape, even though he had witnessed it with his own eyes. But then again, he should know better than to doubt his sister—his brilliant, wonderful sister.

True that he didn't quite know what she meant with the whole flower business, and he still wasn't sure what was up with her talking to herself. Though, if he had to be honest, Goldenrod had always been a little eccentric. Then again, it could have all been a part of her grander scheme. And it had worked, hadn't it?

Of course it had! And wouldn't it just be for the best if he ignored the fact that she seemed to be muttering to herself even now? Birch stole a side-glance at Goldenrod as he continued to run alongside her and then decided to turn his attention elsewhere.

Like on how fine everything was. His sister wasn't crazy. They were going to get out of these woods perfectly safe and sound. And he, Birch Awl Moram, was going to happily spend the rest of his summer vacation relishing the boredom. He was going to wade in boredom until his fingers got pruney and never attempt anything as ridiculous as an adventure again.

He could almost see the edge of the woods now. He started to run faster toward the beautiful, unfiltered light, toward certain freedom.

Then, he heard the sound of snapping twigs and a drawling voice laughing almost directly to his right. Goldenrod must have heard it too because Birch immediately felt her grab his backpack and pull him down behind a bush.

They had been only moments away from running smack dab into Toe Jam and No-Bone.

No-Bone was sweating. He had used the fifty dollars he'd weaseled out of that supremely gullible chiropractor to buy a camel-colored faux-leather jacket. It was entirely too hot to be wearing it, but he thought it looked too cool to take it off. He had never had anything like it when he was traveling with the circus or at the orphanage afterward. He particularly liked the way it stretched along with him as he maneuvered his body into all of its impossible positions.

No-Bone had a very vague recollection of his dad owning a leather jacket similar to it. It was one of the few pictures he could conjure up in his mind of his parents, both sitting atop a shiny, chrome motorcycle. It's possible the image in his head was from the morning before the accident. Or maybe his imagination had just dramatized it in that way.

He was six when the accident happened and knew enough about himself to be violently against being sent to an orphanage. Back when his parents were still alive, whenever he threw a tantrum, his father would say, "If you don't like it here, why don't you run away and join a circus?"

So when he was standing at the train platform with his temporary guardian, looking up at the colorful sign for the Orange & Clyde Big Top Act, it seemed to him like, well, a sign. All No-Bone had to do was dodge his guardian for a minute, take the train from the other platform, and then eventually tell his sob story to a few clowns who would convince the ringmaster to let them keep him.

Of course, that's where he had learned to maneuver his spine. Xiao, the head acrobat, had taken notice almost right away when he'd spied No-Bone trying to fit himself into the circus bus's luggage rack. At first, No-Bone had thought that the small, fierce-looking man had come to yell at him, and he'd quickly tumbled off the rack and tried to run away. But once Xiao had caught up with him—which incidentally was in about two seconds, in case you ever have the bright idea to try and flee from a top acrobat—he'd gently put his hand on No-Bone's shoulder and simply said, "You've got talent. Would you like to learn more about how to use it?"

From there, the lessons had begun, and No-Bone had spent hours and hours practicing everything from tumbles and somersaults to high-flying, gravity-defying trapeze tricks. His proudest moment came at the age of seven when he officially became the youngest performer to ever grace the Orange & Clyde stage.

No-Bone had been heartbroken when the show was forced to pack up. He was nine, and Xiao was going back to China. The clowns and lion tamers and all the various other friends he had made all had their own lives to get to and work to find. So he had wound up in an orphanage anyway, here in boring, old Pilmilton. Sure, he enjoyed winning limbo competitions, but he had to believe there were bigger and better things out there for a boy of his talents. That's what Spitbubble had promised him anyway: some excitement.

"I'm bored," Toe Jam said as if he could read No-Bone's thoughts. "How come I never get to be in on any of the plans?" He kicked some dirt with the tip of his expensive sneakers.

No-Bone smirked. It was true that Toe Jam really had no part in tomorrow's proceedings, whereas he, No-Bone, would be a star player. Teasingly, he said, "Come on. You really wanna get involved with that stuff? This way we do all the work, and you get all the benefits." As he spoke, No-Bone went out of his way to bend backward underneath a particularly low tree branch.

"I guess," Toe Jam sulked. "But I wanna do *something*. What about all that adventure Spitbubble is always talking about? What about being a hoodlum?"

No-Bone had straightened up again to his neutral C posture. He thought for a moment. "Well, if you really wanna do something, I have an idea. And it'll impress Spitbubble and the others too."

Toe Jam's face immediately brightened. "What is it?"

"You know that old lady who lives at the edge of the woods?"

"Yeah?" he said hesitantly.

"Well," No-Bone casually drawled out, "everyone says she keeps a load of cash under her mattress 'cause she doesn't trust banks."

"Who's everyone?" Toe Jam asked skeptically.

"I don't know. Everyone. I just heard it, okay?"

"How d'you know it's true?"

"I don't . . . but there's only one way to find out," No-Bone said.

Toe Jam remained quiet.

"We break into her house, you idiot," No-Bone said.

"Yeah, I get where you're going," Toe Jam immediately retorted. "I just don't know if it's such a good idea . . . ," he trailed off.

"Dude, all I've heard you do all day is complain about not doing anything. And now I'm giving us something to do . . . and you don't wanna? *What about being a hoodlum?*" No-Bone mimicked Toe Jam in a high singsongy voice. Sometimes, it was just too easy to goad this rich kid who had never had to worry about getting enough food or Christmas presents a day in his life.

Toe Jam punched him on the arm. "Stop."

"*Stop*," No-Bone continued in the same voice.

Out of nowhere, his head cocked down like a bull's, Toe Jam rammed into No-Bone's curved middle. Both of them fell into a heap on the floor.

All right, so maybe No-Bone had underestimated the richie's fighting skills. After all, he probably had a private wrestling ring or something in that giant mansion of his. Still, he thought, very little could actually be a match for his stupendously amazing spine tricks. And to prove this point, he started to curve his body around Toe Jam's limbs like a snake.

TOUGHER, STRONGER, GROSSER

The rosebush was exactly where the girl had said it would be, but Snotshot was eyeing it suspiciously anyway.

In retrospect, it had probably been pretty stupid to let the girl and her brother go. She had to admit, as weak as the girl seemed like she might be physically, she had proven herself to be rather on the smart side. This had all probably been some trick, and Snotshot was angry at herself for falling for it.

After all, a flower? Really? What a stupid, girly thing to be after. She looked skeptically at the lush blue roses sprouting all over the bush. She had probably passed this bush hundreds of times and had never even noticed it before. That's because she didn't have time for flowers. Or anything else, really, that a girl her age was supposedly meant to fawn over.

When Spitbubble had come upon Snotshot in the woods, a few days after she had run away from home for good, he had thought he could bully her just because she was a girl. All the kids had, really. She had been forced to prove them wrong. She had had to be just as loud, just as tough, and just as gross as any of them. Louder, tougher, and grosser if possible. That's why she had chosen the special "talent" that she had. The boogers were enough to make all the boys cringe, even Toe Jam, who was hands down the least likely to be found within a ten-foot radius of a shower.

Luckily, her ex-home life had prepared her for all of this: being tough and being independent. She didn't want to think about that, though. She had gotten herself out of her old life, and she wasn't going back. Instead, she focused on the plant in front of her.

Looking around to make sure no one was in sight to witness it, Snotshot bent down to take a small whiff. Immediately, a rush of memories flooded her. Suddenly, she was five years old and digging a hole on a sandy beach. The hole was big and round and perfect, and close enough to the ocean that the bottom of it had filled with cool, salty water. She and her dad were dipping their feet into it, and there was a wild, crazy sound in the air. She soon realized it was the sound of her own laughing, a carefree and ringing laugh that she hadn't even remembered she had. This was all before, of course. Before her mom had left and her dad had become so sad that it was impossible to live with him.

Her breath caught in her chest, and Snotshot was suddenly whipped back to her present-day reality. She shook her head, wanting to shake herself free of the memory she had just unwittingly happened upon. *No,* she thought. *It isn't any good to think of those days. They're gone, and I have to move forward. Tougher and stronger. And grosser, when necessary.*

Even better, wealthy, if possible. Gently, since she didn't want to damage her possible treasure trove and since she had spotted some nasty-looking thorns on the flower's stem, Snotshot held a rose by its bud as she used the shears the girl had given her to cut it. She placed it carefully in the old jam jar. Then she cut another and another. The jam jar would only hold five, so she left the other few on the bush as they were.

She closed the jar lid tight, just as directed, and she looked at the flowers through the glass. They seemed to give off a faint glow, almost like weak blue Christmas lights.

She held the jar low by her side as she walked back toward the cavern. She didn't think it was necessary to share this discovery with anyone else. For one thing, there was no need for anyone to know that she had even seen the two kids after the big idiot let them escape.

For another, if the girl had been right and the flowers were worth a lot of money—a possibility that despite her natural skepticism, she realized she was inclined to believe— well then, why should she have to share that with anyone?

A DUSTY DISCOVERY

Goldenrod knew Meriwether was not happy with her. He had made that much abundantly clear during his reappearance before they had almost run into Toe Jam and No-Bone.

After listening to a brief lecture from the ghost, which by the way proved to be just as frustrating as a lecture from any solid adult, Goldenrod had pleaded her case to him. What was she supposed to have done? Not only was it the only way she had thought of to get her and Birch safely away from the clutches of Spitbubble's gang but, she pointed out, it was also the only way she had thought of to get the rose cut in time. After all, it was either today or another whole fifty years.

Meriwether didn't have much of a response to that.

"Believe me, I want to get it back as much as you do,"

Goldenrod had told him. "And I promise I'll try to come up with a way."

He had muttered something that sounded like, "Well, you know where to find me. Looks like I'll be here another half a century," before vanishing again.

She needed to come up with a plan to reclaim the blue rose, but that would have to wait. Because once again, she had another more pressing matter bothering her.

The Morams had seized the opportunity and noise Toe Jam and No-Bone's impromptu wrestling match had caused to make another attempt at running out of the forest. Finally, they could see the sun streaming through the edge of the woods. They were almost home, and Goldenrod could see Birch break out into a wide grin.

She was sorry to do it, but she had to at least tell him where she was going. She grabbed on to his backpack. "Hey," she panted. "Listen, I have to warn the old lady." She pointed in the direction of the cottage that could now be clearly glimpsed from between the trees. "Before I go home."

"Who is she?" Birch asked.

"She's my friend. She lives in there. I have to tell her what we overheard, but I understand if you want to just go home," Goldenrod said.

Birch looked extremely reluctant. Goldenrod could almost see the wheels turning in his head about whether to brave the rest of the way home by himself or to at least stick with his sister, even though she was choosing to go on yet another mission that didn't involve the safety of their house.

He sighed, but nodded and pointed toward the cottage.

Goldenrod gave a small smile. "Come on. We'll make it quick." She led the way up the path of the brilliant little garden, to the porch with the metal table and chairs, and to the front door.

She knocked.

There was no answer. Birch nervously looked in the direction of the forest.

Goldenrod knocked again.

Still no answer. Birch grabbed the buckle on his backpack and started to squeeze it.

On the third knock, the door to the old lady's house swung open a tiny bit.

"Oh, great . . . she doesn't even lock the door? Those jerks are gonna have it so easy," Goldenrod mumbled as she pushed the door open a bit more and peeked around the corner.

It was only at this moment, when Goldenrod went to call out the old lady's name, that she realized she didn't know it. She was surprised at herself. *What sort of Legendary Adventurer wouldn't gather all the facts?* she thought.

"Hello?" she finally called out. "Anyone home? It's Goldenrod."

She stepped a little farther into the house.

"Are you sure this is okay?" Birch asked.

"Yes. I told you, she's my friend," Goldenrod said as she walked farther into the room and Birch followed.

The house was dark. All the shades were drawn. And as Birch quickly closed the front door, the room grew darker still. It took a few moments for their eyes to adjust to the dimness. At first, all they could see was an abundance of dust dancing in the light leaking out of the closed blinds. But slowly, they began to realize that the dust wasn't just dancing there; it absolutely permeated everything in the little house.

Goldenrod, who now also realized that she had never before set foot in the old lady's house (she was very mad at herself for having missed so many details—Meriwether Lewis would probably be even more appalled with her than he already was), was aghast. If she didn't know any better, she would say that no one had lived in the cottage for years.

The front room was also the only room on the first floor. It seemed to serve as a living room, dining room, and small kitchen all at once. But everything, from the old wooden furniture to the picture frames on the mantelpiece, was covered with a layer of dust thick enough to obscure all details (like the exact color of the wood or the faces of the people in the photos). There was one small exception. The thin pink runner rug that ran from the front door to the kitchen seemed to be immaculate, as was a tiny space on the kitchen counter, which Goldenrod could now see housed the china teacups that she had once been served chocolate milk in.

The little details Goldenrod could make out through all the thick gray fuzz were odd. Crocheted shawls, black-and-white photographs, old needlepoint samplers. Everything seemed like a cliché of an old lady's house, like things that someone with no imagination would automatically assume belonged in one.

"Hello?" Goldenrod called again, a little less certain. There was still no answer.

"I don't think she's here," Birch said meekly, clearly wanting to go home.

But Goldenrod had just noticed that the pristine pink runner ended at the bottom of the staircase—which was also completely dust-free.

Without hesitation, she immediately made her way over and started to climb the stairs.

"Goldenrod . . . ," Birch began. She motioned for him to follow her. His face set into a severe expression of worry; he bit his lip and obeyed.

At the top of the stairs was a long hallway, off of which stood one door to either side and one door straight at the end, all of which were shut.

Goldenrod creaked straight down the hallway and to the last door. She reached for the knob.

"Goldenrod." Birch had finally found his voice again. "Can we please just go home? Please?"

Goldenrod turned around to him. "She's my friend, Birch. I have to warn her about No-Bone and Toe Jam."

"Can't you call her from home?"

"I don't have her number."

"But Mom . . ."

"Oh, Birch," Goldenrod sighed. "I wish you were a little braver."

Birch dropped his head but didn't say anything.

"Let's just make sure she's not here, and then we'll go, okay?"

"Fine," Birch said.

Goldenrod turned the knob and opened the door.

It was as if she had stepped into an entirely different house. The room was large and airy. There was a beautiful snow-white carpet on the ground and a large mahogany four-poster in the middle. On the nightstand, there was a cell phone plugged into the wall.

On one side of the room was a large and handsome dresser. On the opposite wall stood a matching vanity table, which was neatly set with a wide variety of glass perfume bottles. Next to this was a sleek, shiny, and seemingly brand-new computer.

Goldenrod couldn't help but gape. This modern, immaculately spotless bedroom seemed to have nothing in common with the rest of the house. For a moment, she even forgot what she was supposed to be doing there. She walked over to the dresser, peeked into the top drawer, and found what must have been the most neatly folded sock drawer in the history of mankind.

"She's not here," Birch said hopefully.

But just then, Goldenrod noticed that she was standing underneath a large square tile on the ceiling. The tile had caught her eye because hanging from it was a big and ornate brass handle.

There was no way she'd be able to reach the handle on her own, so she looked around for something to stand on. The computer chair would work just fine. She pushed it over, stood on it, and pulled on the handle. The tile swung open and down came a metal ladder with it.

What sort of explorer would see a ladder and not want to climb up it? Goldenrod's mind very logically asked. *Not this sort,* she thought with just a hint of glee as she put her foot on the first rung. Besides, how was she supposed to get to the bottom of the mystery of the old lady if she didn't gather every clue that she could find?

23

THE ATTIC

Birch looked on, horrified.

"It's an attic." Goldenrod sounded delighted as she started to climb up the ladder.

She had just poked her head past the ceiling when Birch immediately heard her give a sharp intake of breath. "Whoa!" she said.

"What?" Birch asked, afraid of the answer.

"You have to come see this," she said as she stepped all the way up the ladder and disappeared into the ceiling door.

Birch really didn't want to go up the ladder. But, at that moment, he decided to try very hard to grant his older sister's wish that he be braver. After all, he couldn't expect her to include him in her activities if he couldn't even act courageous in the face of an attic. With a sigh, he cautiously made his way over to the middle of the room, stepped onto the chair, and then onto the first rung. He had never been on a ladder before, and it wasn't such a pleasant experience. Still, slowly, he made his way up.

He didn't stop looking at the rungs until he had his feet on solid ground again. Only then was he able to take in where he was and give the same sharp intake of breath he had heard from Goldenrod.

The room was absolutely crammed with *stuff*—some of it protected by plastic bags, some things large, some things smaller, but almost all of it shiny. There were very few things in the room that didn't look like they were made out of gold or silver: trophies, goblets, large scrolled mirrors, sets of silverware.

Birch walked over to Goldenrod, who was examining a silver mirror closely. At first, he thought she was frowning at the green and brown makeup that was still on her face and now streaked with little rivulets of sweat. But then he realized that it was actually the back of the mirror that she was staring at. "What is all this?" he asked her.

Goldenrod looked up at Birch, seeming troubled. "I don't know," she said. "But look at this."

She showed him an engraved design on the back of the mirror. It looked like a shield and had two crossed telescopes and some sort of bird on it. A banner across the bird's tail spelled out the word "Lewis."

"What is that?" Birch asked.

"It's Randy Lewis-O'Malley's family crest. I've seen it before on his backpack. And it seems to be on a lot of things around here . . ." She looked at all the shiny engraved items surrounding them.

"Who's Randy Lewis-O'Malley?" Birch asked.

"Toe Jam," Goldenrod said slowly. "So what is *she* doing with all of *his* family's stuff?"

But just then, Goldenrod's eyes widened in shock. Birch watched as she walked, almost as if in a trance, toward what was probably the dullest thing in the room: a small, framed and dusty illustration of a bird, labeled in someone's old-fashioned handwriting. Goldenrod picked it up, stared at it, and muttered, "I don't believe it . . ."

"What?" Birch asked, going over to see the drawing closer.

It looked like the same bird that appeared on Toe Jam's family crest, but he couldn't see what was so special about it.

"This is his woodpecker. Meriwether Lewis's. Look!" Goldenrod pointed to the crammed handwriting, which did, indeed, say "Lewis's Woodpecker (*Melanerpes lewis*), Discovered 1804 by M.L. & W.C."

"But then that means . . . Randy Lewis-O'Malley is related to *him*?!" Goldenrod looked positively distraught.

"Who's Meriwether Lewis?" Birch asked.

Unfortunately, Goldenrod didn't have time to answer, as right then they heard someone opening the front door.

✳

Goldenrod looked up from the picture to see Birch staring at her with a horrified expression. She knew this was exactly the kind of thing he was afraid would happen as soon as he had followed her up the stairs. For once, she almost wished she had allowed his sense of caution to stop her from being so thorough with her explorations. But it was too late now.

As fascinating and slightly horrifying as it was to have discovered what kind of relations Meriwether Lewis had left behind, Goldenrod realized this was not the time to ponder too heavily on it.

She carefully set the picture down, then put her finger to her lips and mouthed a "shhhh . . ." As slowly as she possibly could, she tiptoed toward the ladder and tried to pull it up. It was much heavier than she had expected.

Downstairs, she could hear creaks as someone made their way up the staircase. She heard that someone humming an old-fashioned song, one that she had heard tinkled in every ballerina music box known to man.

It was the old lady. Although just five minutes ago Goldenrod had been hoping they would meet so that she could warn her, now she was a bit disturbed by everything she had seen. What was she doing with all of Randy's stuff? And how come her house was so weird?

She decided the best thing to do would be to hide in the attic—at least until she could come up with a better plan. She motioned for Birch to help her with the ladder.

His tiny muscles weren't a huge boost but—combined with the sheer Moram determination—they were enough to finally heave the ladder up and shut the tile door behind it. Miraculously, this did not make nearly as much noise as Goldenrod had feared it would, the door closing with a muted thud as they were almost thrown back with the momentum of it.

They panted as footsteps walked up the hallway and to the bedroom door.

"Oh, my, my. I left the bedroom door open? Perhaps Edward is right about me," they heard the old lady mutter and then laugh lightly to herself.

She entered the bedroom and started to shuffle around in it.

Birch was biting his lower lip and looking down at the floor, as if by doing so he could actually see what the old lady was up to, and Goldenrod found herself wishing that they both could. She carefully scooted over to Birch and put one arm around his shoulder. He looked up at her, and she tried her best to smile with confidence, even though she clearly had no idea what she was doing.

From the bedroom, they heard the sound of the computer being turned on.

The old lady continued to sing. She had now moved on

to an operatic rendition of a pop song that had recently hit the radio and featured the lyrics, "Go round and round like the wheels on the bus. Shake it like you're a tot in Toys'R'Us."

Just as soon as the old lady had finished the verse, Goldenrod heard the real song start up. She was confused until she heard the old lady say, "Hello?" and realized that the song must also be the old lady's ringtone.

There was a pause and then the old lady gave a loud sigh. "Not the coin!"

There was another pause.

"Eight hundred dollars? Are you serious?" They could hear the old lady tapping away in annoyance on her computer keys. "No, no. Of course I want it," she said irritably. "That boy has no sense of history." Another pause, and then the old lady said coldly, "Thank you, Barnes. Disciplinary advice from you is always refreshing. Just hold it until tomorrow. I'll be there to pick it up then."

Goldenrod and Birch both looked at each other, Goldenrod now even more disturbed than before. Clearly whatever was going on in the woods, the old lady had some part in it.

The thing was, if Meriwether Lewis was a ghost haunting the woods, and if the old lady was up here holding all of his stuff . . . maybe Goldenrod's original thoughts when she had met the old lady were right and she *was* a witch. After all, if there could be ghosts, who says there couldn't be witches? And maybe somehow she was responsible for conjuring Meriwether up. Or even trapping him in the forest to begin with.

Goldenrod swallowed hard. It couldn't be, though. She had liked the old lady so much. She'd been so nice to Goldenrod and told her all about the blue rose and sent her on a quest. A quest that, she reminded herself, technically would free Meriwether's spirit. On the other hand, the quest had proven to be quite dangerous, and maybe that wasn't such a good thing after all.

As she was pondering this latest mystery, suddenly she heard the sound of the front door being opened once more.

The old lady became very quiet beneath them, and Goldenrod and Birch strained to hear the new intruders.

At first they couldn't make out much, but then came the unmistakable voice of No-Bone.

"Why are you whispering?" he boomed as he made his way up the stairs.

"She might be home," trailed Toe Jam's much quieter voice.

"So . . . what, you and I can't take on a hundred-year-old lady?"

With horror, Goldenrod suddenly noticed that the ladder that was lying flat in front of them was quickly slipping away. Down, down, down it went as the ceiling tile opened once more.

Step-by-step, the old lady climbed up it with a speed and agility that was surprising for someone of her age. She only looked up when she had reached the top.

She had to cover her mouth so as not to cry out, looking startled by the unexpected presence of an oddly colored Goldenrod and a small boy who was cowering into her arm.

TO GRANDMOTHER'S HOUSE WE GO

Goldenrod gave a wan smile. "Um, hi," she whispered awkwardly.

The old lady took her hand down from her mouth.

Goldenrod didn't know what to say or even how to react. An hour ago, she had been sure the old lady was her friend, and then a minute ago, she had been contemplating the possibilities of her being a witch. Although the more she looked into the familiar, though still rather ugly, eyes of the old woman, the more she remembered her own more positive feelings. With Birch pressed against her, Goldenrod could only think of one thing to say in the midst of her confusion. "This is my brother, Birch."

Before the old lady could respond, the creaking from downstairs reminded them all where they were.

"We need to look for something heavy," the old lady

said, and then proceeded to carefully examine the heaps of shiny objects that were all around them.

Goldenrod felt guilty about being found in the old lady's attic this way and started to look around too. There were lots of heavy metal things, including many trophies, and then a few random things also—like a very old baseball and some sort of dusty black cape.

"Never mind," the old lady finally whispered. "I think I found the perfect thing." She was holding an enormous gold trophy in her left hand as if it were featherlight. Birch looked up at her in wonder.

"Uncle Stewie's Kentucky Derby trophy. Never much liked the old man. He used to give me hard candy as a birthday present." She rolled her eyes and then, noticing Birch's awe-filled expression, she added, "Don't worry, kid. I was a champion shot-putter. In fact, those are my Olympic gold medals just behind you."

As Birch turned around to look, they suddenly heard a great deal of noise coming from downstairs. It sounded as if someone was tearing the old lady's bed apart.

"Your mattress. They think you're hiding a wad of cash under it," Goldenrod whispered urgently, only then remembering what she was doing there to begin with.

"What do they think this is . . . the twentieth century?" the old lady asked as she shook her head. "Well, come on, then."

Quietly she crept over to the door in the floor, grabbing the old dirt-and-ink-smeared baseball in her other hand as she passed by. "Hold that ladder while I open the door," she whispered to Goldenrod.

Goldenrod did as she was told. As the old lady quietly inched the door open, Goldenrod fed the ladder to her so that when it finally hit the ground, it did so with barely a small bump. And as Toe Jam and No-Bone were deep in the middle of a loud discussion about why on earth someone would take the time to fold their sheets under the mattress, they didn't hear the old lady tiptoe down the ladder (in a surprising display of dexterity considering that she had both of her hands full), until she stood in front of them and yelled, "Freeze, you good-for-nothing scoundrels."

At first, No-Bone and Toe Jam looked, of course, completely startled. But as soon as No-Bone saw the old lady ridiculously holding a trophy and an old baseball, he started to laugh. "Freeze . . . or . . . or what?" He was laughing so hard it was difficult to get the words out.

Suddenly there was a flash of white, and No-Bone stopped laughing almost immediately. He doubled over (or in his case, quadrupled over), screaming, and dropped the quilt he had been holding up. The old lady had thrown the baseball, hard, and it had hit him in his elbow.

"That's the strength of the 1927 Yankees for you," the old lady said drily. "And you!" She turned suddenly to Toe

Jam. "Don't think I won't sacrifice your Great-Great-Uncle Stewie's trophy to teach you a lesson, you ungrateful piece of toe jam."

Toe Jam's jaw opened so wide that Goldenrod, perched high above with her head poking out to catch all the action, could actually see all the way to his molars.

"Grandma . . . ," he finally managed to breathe out.

"Don't you Grandma me, Randall. I know every single thing you've been up to. And I've been stupid to sit idly by and think you'd be smart enough to get yourself out of it."

Up on their perch, Goldenrod and Birch stared at each other, both of their mouths now also hanging open at the bizarre turns of events.

"And how dare you sell off all the family heirlooms to finance your little hooligan enterprise? Do you have any idea what these things are worth? And I don't mean in cash but in sentimental value?" the old lady continued to yell.

"No one at home has missed them . . . ," Toe Jam answered sheepishly.

"Well, of course not. I don't expect that self-absorbed son of mine and that society wife of his to notice anything. They're too busy tanning and trying to one-up the other country club morons to even realize that they have a son they haven't paid attention to in years."

Randy was stunned into silence. No-Bone, who was still rubbing his sore elbow, seemed to have little to contribute to the conversation either, although he looked just as mesmer-ized by the turn of events as Goldenrod and Birch were. So much so, that his spine finally seemed to be frozen into one position.

"Well, no more, Randall. From now on I'm doing what I should have done from the beginning. Since I actually care about you, you are grounded. You are banned from entering that forest again until you're eighteen years old."

"But I'm only eleven now—" Randy started.

"Exactly," the old lady said emphatically, before turning to No-Bone. "As for you, I'm sure you don't have any parents of your own, do you?"

Still dumbfounded, No-Bone shook his head.

"Well, that seems to be typical for Spitbubble," the old lady said. "But believe me, I have ways to make your life just as sorry as Randall's is going to be."

No-Bone didn't respond, but he certainly looked like he wouldn't want to experiment with her claim.

"Now you're going to tell me where the rest of your miserable lot is," she continued.

No-Bone remained silent.

The old lady positioned the trophy to send it flying at his other arm.

"Okay, okay," he finally said, looking as sore as his elbow. "They decided to teach that Mold-and-rot a lesson. They're at her house."

"Doing what?" the old lady asked.

"Well, apparently Brains knew that Mold-and-rot's mother—"

"Her name isn't Mold-and-rot," the old lady snapped.

No-Bone looked confused, and Goldenrod realized he must have never known her real name. "Oh . . . ," he said.

"It's Goldenrod," Randy squeaked.

"So what did Jonas know about Goldenrod's mother?" the old lady continued.

"Well, he says that she has a really nice garden that she loves, so he was going to—"

"No!" Goldenrod watched with surprise as her little brother went flying down the ladder.

No-Bone and Toe Jam both looked shocked to see him. "You're here?" No-Bone asked stupidly.

Goldenrod supposed that Birch had had it. Between getting kidnapped, and being called names, and hiding in strange, musty attics with curiously strong old ladies, it seemed his tolerance for fear had broken through the threshold. Now, he looked simply angry.

"You, you . . . ," he sputtered as he stamped toward the bigger boys. "You!" he finally screamed as he punched No-Bone in his hurt arm.

"Ow!" No-Bone looked furious. "I'm gonna . . ."

"You will do nothing," the old lady boomed, "or I will call the cops."

By this point, Goldenrod had climbed down the ladder and was standing beside Birch.

"Let's go stop him, Birch," she said.

Birch turned to her, and Goldenrod saw a look of determination and confidence she had never, ever seen on his face before. Her heart surged with pride.

"Okay," he said and immediately started for the door.

"Thanks," Goldenrod told the old lady before jogging after him. "Wait," she stopped just as she had gotten to the front door. "What's your name?" She turned to the old lady.

"Cassandra Rubina Lewis." The old lady stood up a little straighter as she said it. "Pleased to meet you, and you'd better hurry."

SOMETHING EVIL

Goldenrod and Birch were running faster than they ever had in their lives. Each was conjuring up a different horrific vision of what they might find when they finally got back to their house.

Birch was imagining a front lawn that resembled the color of severely rusted iron. The sun would blaze on the penny-colored grass, sharply outlining the wilted brown petals of all his mother's flowers. A tumbleweed would roll by as a whistling tune played.

Okay, so that's probably not exactly how it would go, but Birch was imagining the worst.

As they got nearer and nearer to their house, Birch could feel the pit of his stomach stretch farther and farther down toward his feet. He was almost dreading this moment more than anything else that had happened to him all day.

Finally, they turned the corner onto their street and could see their green roof at the end of the block. Little by little, as they passed each neighboring home, more of their house came into view. First the white sidings. Then the windows. The front door. And, finally, they caught a glimpse of their lawn.

It was green. As green as their roof. As green as it had ever been.

Birch could hardly believe it. Maybe they weren't too late after all . . . he could see the purples of some of the dahlias, the tall goldenrods, the chrysanthemums, and all the rest. And there, happily spraying them, was his mother, in her orange gardening gloves and clogs. She was humming to herself.

Goldenrod ran to her. But, as overjoyed as Birch was to see no damage done, he also quickly remembered that he was probably in trouble. He couldn't see how it would be possible, but he hung back behind Goldenrod, hoping that she might create some distraction that would make their mother forget he was supposed to be sick in bed. At least she was wearing some crazy face paint. That might help.

"Mom!" Goldenrod yelled breathlessly.

Their mother looked up. "Hello, darling," she said cheerfully. "What's that on your face?"

"Oh. Right. I was just practicing my camouflage techniques."

Mrs. Moram looked like she was thinking this through for a moment before shrugging it off with a smile. "Oh."

It figures that it'd take more than face paint to bother her, Birch thought with a sigh.

"So . . . is everything all right?" Goldenrod asked.

"What do you mean?" Mrs. Moram squinted as she looked up at her daughter in the late-afternoon sun.

"I mean, has anything been destroyed . . . or, er, anyone strange visited here?" Goldenrod seemed to be faltering.

Their mother was staring at her and looking slightly confused. "No, of course not, dear. Are *you* okay?"

Goldenrod nodded.

"Are you sure?" their mother continued. "You look a little flushed. I hope you're not coming down with whatever it is that Birch has."

The moment she said his name, she noticed her son standing back at the edge of the lawn. "What are you doing out of bed?" she asked.

Birch gulped, thinking that it was finally time to come clean.

"Are you feeling better, dear?" Mrs. Moram followed brightly. She got up and walked over to him, took one hand out of a bright orange glove, and went to feel Birch's forehead. "Hmmm . . . you're a little warm."

"I'm better," Birch said meekly.

"Hmmm . . . well, yes. You are looking a little less pale."

"I'll, um, take him inside, Mom," Goldenrod said.

"Okay, dear. I'm almost finished out here. I'll be inside in a minute."

Goldenrod gently took Birch by the shoulder and led him through the front door.

As soon as they had gotten inside, she started frantically running around the house, looking under the tables, in all the drawers, and in every nook and cranny she came across.

"What are you doing?" Birch asked.

"We were gone so long," Goldenrod said. "Brains must have already been here. Don't you think?"

"But what are you looking for?"

"I have no idea. Knowing him, something pretty evil."

With a sharp nod, Birch also started to search the house, hoping that he'd be able to spot evil items fast enough to prevent them from causing damage.

They had made their way through the front hallway and living room, not leaving a single coaster or souvenir plate unturned. They were about to start on the kitchen when they heard their mother calling Goldenrod's name.

Goldenrod went to the front door to answer.

"Could you grab me another bottle of insecticide?" their mother's voice came drifting into the house. "There's one in the box on the kitchen counter."

"Sure," Goldenrod said and walked over to a small cardboard box that was, in fact, on the kitchen counter. She took a small, white spray bottle from it. But instead of walking the bottle out to her mother, she seemed to completely freeze.

After she hadn't moved for a few moments, Birch started toward her. "What's the matter?" he asked, noting Goldenrod's wide-eyed look of horror as she stared down into the box.

Slowly, she turned the white spray bottle around. There was a label on it with bright red writing. BRAINS'S ALL-ORGANIC GARDEN INSECTICIDE, it said. THE ENVIRONMENT-FRIENDLY SOLUTION TO ALL YOUR PESKIEST PROBLEMS. In tiny writing in the corner were the words: A TRADEMARK OF SPITBUBBLE, INC. There was a picture of a hand giving the thumbs-up right next to a plump red rose.

They stared at each other in horror for only a moment, before both bolting straight for the front door.

There, they saw their mother liberally spraying her garden with the other white bottle.

"Mom . . ." Goldenrod ran up to her breathlessly. "Where did you get this?" She showed her mother the bottle that was in her hand.

"Oh, it was a free gift from the Seed of the Month Club. It's supposed to be amazing. Look at all these testimonials on the back. From *Home & Garden* and everything." She went to grab the bottle out of Goldenrod's hand, but Goldenrod wouldn't let go.

"How much of it did you use?" Goldenrod asked.

"The first sampler bottle. I used it on the entire lawn. It's supposed to be good for grass too." Mrs. Moram tugged on the bottle.

Birch looked hopelessly around the lawn. Now that he knew, he could see how all of it seemed to glisten in a rather peculiar way.

"Goldenrod, dear, you have quite the firm grip." Mrs. Moram kept tugging.

"Um, don't use the rest, Mom," Birch said.

"Why not?" Mrs. Moram looked confused.

"Because . . . because, the directions say not to use more than one bottle per week," Birch blurted out.

"They do?" Mrs. Moram frowned, holding up her empty bottle to read the label.

"Yup," Goldenrod said brightly. "Let me throw that out for you." She grabbed the other bottle out of her mother's hand and walked back into the house, Birch right behind her. They both looked at each other with eerily identical narrowed eyes.

26

PLOTTING OVER CHOCOLATE MILK

When Goldenrod walked into the living room the next morning, a little earlier even than she usually set out, her dad had just left for work and her mom was tending to the small herb garden they had on their kitchen sill.

"Hi, Mom," Goldenrod said.

"Morning. Would you like some breakfast?" She went to open the cereal cupboard.

"No, I don't think so," Goldenrod said. "I packed something. I just wanted to ask if it would be okay if I took Birch with me today?"

"Oh. Is he feeling well enough, you think?"

"Yeah, I feel fine," Birch said as he entered the kitchen. "I really would like to go outside with Goldenrod. I feel like I was cooped up all day yesterday . . ." Which, if Birch had to justify it, was definitely sort of the truth.

"Okay. I suppose some fresh air might be good. But walk him right back home if he starts feeling sick, Goldenrod, okay?"

Goldenrod nodded and she and Birch left the house. They both looked carefully at their front lawn as they walked past it. It still seemed as perfect as ever, though Goldenrod thought she saw a slight wilt to some of the stems and stalks.

The night before, Goldenrod had gone into Birch's room and they had had a little chat about everything that had happened. And beyond being scared, beyond being upset, they had realized that they were both very angry. It wasn't fair that these bullies could just get away with everything.

There was one—okay, never mind—there were *many* problems. But the most glaring one was that they were just two kids against a massively sinister gang. They didn't want to hurt anyone, and they didn't really want to get in trouble. But they weren't very happy sitting back and doing nothing either.

Privately, Goldenrod had another issue eating away at her. She had to figure out a way to get the blue rose back from under Snotshot's indelicate claws.

After a lot of consideration, Goldenrod had suggested they ask for help from the old lady. It was true that Goldenrod still didn't quite know what to think of her involvement in everything and whether she could fully be trusted. Undoubtedly, however, Cassandra Lewis was the one adult who would at least understand the significance of the blue rose. Besides which, Goldenrod realized, she had never even had the chance to tell her that she'd actually found it.

So the cottage was where they were heading now, walking quickly because it was the first of many things on their to-do list for the day. When they got there, they decided to knock on the door this time.

The old lady opened it and immediately let them inside.

"Come in, come in. Straight to the back. Randall is here." She led them through the dusty kitchen and into a back room that had glass walls on three sides of it with massive rosebushes clinging to each one. At the center of the wooden floor was a green metallic table and matching chairs—more lawn furniture, Goldenrod noted. It was almost like being in a greenhouse. Toe Jam sat on one of the chairs. His face had been scrubbed clean, and he had a china cup of chalky chocolate milk in front of him.

Cassandra followed them in with two more flowered china cups. She poured each of them some chocolate milk.

"Randall, did you say hello?" she asked sternly.

"Hi," Randy sulked.

"Well . . . what happened?" She turned to Goldenrod and Birch.

"They destroyed our mom's garden—or, at least, it will be destroyed once the poisoned insecticide sets in," Goldenrod said.

The old lady gave a loud sigh. "That Stanley Barbroff is a no-good, dirty—"

"Barbroff?" Goldenrod interjected. "Like, Ms. Barbroff? My fifth-grade teacher?"

"The very one. Stanley is her son," Cassandra said.

"Um, who's Stanley?" Birch asked.

"Stanley Barbroff, aka Spitbubble," Cassandra said.

Goldenrod gave a sharp intake of breath. "Spitbubble is Ms. Barf's *son*?"

Cassandra nodded.

"And—and all those times she warned me about—about turning into a *hoodlum* . . ." Goldenrod was indignant.

"Yes, well, as so often happens with parents, dear, sometimes they can't see their own children for the forest."

"But, she was such a . . . such a . . ." Goldenrod was fuming.

The old lady patted her on the hand. "Believe me, I can imagine what she must be like to have parented *that* conniving criminal."

Randall sniffed loudly at the comment and looked a little miffed.

"What exactly is he doing in the forest anyway?" Goldenrod asked. "I mean, I know they're planning on breaking into the museum or something . . ."

"You've hit the nail pretty much on the head. Spitbubble and his Gross-Out Gang, as they like to call themselves.

Breaking into places, stealing family heirlooms"—she gave a sharp glance at Randy who stared down at his chocolate milk—"and basically creating petty sorts of havoc. Spitbubble himself doesn't do much of it, of course. Like any good leader, he delegates. And like any good dictator, he doesn't exactly have the most savory methods of getting recruits."

"What do you mean?" Goldenrod asked.

"Didn't you ever wonder why those kids could spend all their time in that cavern without anyone noticing?"

The truth was, Goldenrod hadn't. Between not knowing the old lady's name the day before and this, she was once again feeling a little ashamed at her own lack of curiosity.

"It's because most of them don't really have anyone to notice. They're either orphans or maybe just have parents who should pay more attention . . ." At this she stared again at Randy, but this time with a soft gleam in her eye. "But that's what Spitbubble feeds on. He knows these kids have no family, so he gives them one. Of sorts. Only, of course, there's a due for getting in."

"It's not all like that," Toe Jam mumbled. He paused and looked up at his grandmother as if expecting her to cut him off. But she just looked back like she wanted him to continue. "He's not that bad sometimes. He gave some of us a home who didn't have one . . ."

Goldenrod was stunned. She had never, ever thought she would feel sorry for Brains and Lint and all the rest of them. But suddenly, there was a tiny little tugging near her rib cage. "You knew about this?" she finally breathed to the old lady.

Cassandra sighed. "Not all of it. I knew that there were some kids who hung out in there a lot. And I knew that my grandson had started joining them. But I didn't know everything until Randall just told me. The truth is, we come from a long line of explorers, of great men and women who discovered and learned because they were allowed to find their own way out of things. But I let it get too far with Randall."

"So you *are* related to Meriwether Lewis!" Goldenrod exclaimed.

"Yes," Cassandra said. "He would have been my great-great-great-great-great-great-uncle. Our family's crest is—"

"The woodpecker that he discovered and that was named after him," Goldenrod said breathlessly. "I know."

Cassandra looked at Goldenrod with a surprised smile playing at the corners of her lips. "Yes, that's exactly right," she said.

"You know," Goldenrod started, "I was wondering, Mrs. Lewis, if maybe you have any more of those muffins?" She gave the old lady what she hoped was a knowing look.

"Oh, yes, certainly. Would you like to help me get them?" Cassandra stood up at once.

Goldenrod nodded and eagerly followed her to her kitchen. Cassandra made sure to close the door behind them.

"Goldenrod," she said excitedly. "Did you find—"

"The rose?" Goldenrod asked. "I found it . . . but I don't have it. Yet."

Goldenrod explained to her what had happened with Snotshot in the woods. "It was my only bargaining chip," she pleaded when she was done.

Unlike Meriwether, the old lady seemed to have no problem accepting this. "Of course it was. Very few things in the world could be more important than your brother."

Goldenrod was glad at least that Cassandra wasn't going to make her feel guilty. After a moment, she said quietly, "Meriwether told me how important the rose is too." Immediately, she looked up to see the old lady's reaction.

At first Cassandra's expression was hard to read and then, suddenly, she broke out into a giant grin, her crooked teeth leaning every which way. "So you *did* meet him?"

Goldenrod let out a sigh of relief because, after all, this was the first acknowledgment that the ghost wasn't a complete figment of her own imagination. "Yes," she said. "You have too, right?" Again, she carefully examined Cassandra to see if she could pick up on any reaction that might prove or disprove her whole witch theory.

Cassandra kept smiling, but shook her head rather sadly. "I've always wanted to. Especially since he's family and all. But only the person on the quest for the rose can see him, you know. It's part of the family legend."

Her expression was so open and genuine that Goldenrod couldn't help but believe her. So Cassandra wasn't the reason that Meriwether was stuck in the forest after all. "How come you never went on the quest, then?" was her next logical question.

Cassandra sighed. "Well, I missed my chance fifty years ago when *I* was a young girl. I was in college, and my grandmother was the one who told me about the quest. Foolishly, I didn't quite believe her, and I went off on a tour of Europe with my shot-put/a cappella group instead. A youthful mistake."

"But why couldn't you have just gone later? Why couldn't you go now?" Goldenrod asked. Clearly, after seeing all of the displays of the old lady's athletic prowess, she could no longer believe that a thing like arthritis would keep her from doing anything.

"My time has passed," Cassandra said. "Since I refused the quest when it was first offered to me, I would never have been able to find that rosebush again, no matter how many extraordinary maps or compasses or directions I followed. It is simply the way of the quest."

Cassandra cleared her throat. "When you came my way a few weeks ago, I just knew you were the one I was supposed to send on that quest. When Randall was younger, I had wondered if it could be him. But the truth is, he never would have been able to complete it. He would have been like me and deemed it unimportant. But you, you immediately understood just how important it was. You *rose* to the occasion, Goldenrod, and I'm proud of you." The old lady gave a mischievous smile.

Goldenrod beamed.

"All that being said," the old lady continued, "it's possible that I may owe you an apology."

"An apology?" Goldenrod asked.

"Yes. Even if I knew that you were the right person, I still should have considered the consequences. I guess maybe I've gotten a little too old to remember that there often isn't adventure without danger."

Goldenrod chewed on that for a moment. "Don't apologize," she finally said. "That's what I wanted . . . adventure." She looked up at the old woman defiantly. "Now I just have to come up with a way to get the rose back."

Cassandra smiled. "I have a feeling if there's anyone who can do that, it's you. But we should probably be getting back out there or they might think we're doing something truly outrageous in here. Like baking these muffins from scratch," she said as she took another plastic crate of store-bought muffins from a cupboard and walked them out to the little greenhouse room.

Goldenrod followed her as she set them on the table. Birch and Randy weren't speaking to each other. Randy was still staring down at his chocolate milk, not looking

very pleased with himself, while Birch was carefully examining his surroundings.

"Birch, dear," Cassandra asked kindly, "is there something bothering you?"

Birch jumped at being addressed. "Oh . . . no," he said
unconvincingly.

"Are you sure?" Cassandra encouraged.

Birch paused. "It's just . . . well, your house. It's a little . . .
weird." He seemed to blush as soon as he said it. But Goldenrod had to admit, she was just as curious as he was.

She looked eagerly over at Cassandra, who was smiling.
"Yes, I suppose that's as good a word for it as any. Most
of those things"—she waved nonchalantly in the direction of
her dusty first floor—"they were presents from my son,
Edward, Randall's father. We had a bit of a falling out when
I decided to give up the mansions and fancy cars and all that
other nonsense for a nice, quiet life with my garden. My
son takes his revenge the way he deals with anything else in
life—by throwing money at it. I imagine he thought he'd
get me to change my ways if he made me feel as much like
an old lady as possible.

"But I'm nobody if not a girl who likes to mess
around with people's expectations." She winked at Goldenrod. "After all, coming from a long line of explorers also
means coming from a long line of people who don't really
like to be told who to be. So I never go near that stuff, but

keep it around just the same. As a good reminder that I live my life the way I want." Goldenrod saw the old lady peek slyly at her from the corner of her eye.

"Oh," Birch said. He hesitated a moment and then continued quietly, "Actually, there is one more thing we wanted to ask you. Our mother's garden is destroyed and, well, we just don't think it's fair for Spitbubble and the rest of them to get away with it."

"Oh, you don't, eh?" Cassandra gave a little smile.

"Nope. And we want to do something . . . ," Goldenrod said.

"I think," Birch said slowly, "that we want to take them on."

The old lady let out a short cackle. "Well, well . . . I must say, I think that's a splendid idea."

"Only we're not sure exactly what to do," Birch said.

"Don't worry. We'll figure it out together. Randall will help."

Randy scowled into his cup, but for the next hour—with some prodding from his grandmother—he filled them in on all sorts of information that helped them formulate a plan.

A SPOOKY EXPERIMENT

A little bit later on, Goldenrod found herself alone at the edge of the forest once again. She had left Birch, Randy, and Cassandra to deal with some of the finer points of their plan while she conducted a different sort of business.

She carried a replacement backpack, although she had yet to replenish its missing supplies of notebooks, graph paper, and the like. There was a very strong possibility that she would have to make a quick getaway and carrying a lightened load would make that much easier.

When she reached the edge of the forest this time, she cased her surroundings carefully, looking around just like she and Charla had once practiced; it was very important that there would be no kidnappings today. Quickly, she slipped into the forest.

She moved as quietly as she possibly could, all the while

keeping very alert for any signs of Spitbubble or the Gross-Out Gang. Every now and then, when she was positive that there was no one around, she would call out, in as loud a whisper as she dared, "Meriwether!"

So far, she had gotten no response.

Finally, Goldenrod made it over to the little clearing where she had first seen the ghost. After remaining quiet for over five minutes, straining her ears to make sure there were no signs of other human beings, Goldenrod allowed herself to call his name a little louder.

There was still no response.

"I'm on a quest to reclaim the blue rose," Goldenrod said in a firm, but quiet voice.

There was a brief second of silence and then, with a pop, Meriwether appeared in the center of the clearing. He gave a slight bow to Goldenrod, but she could see that he still looked a little grumpy. She wondered if he had been sulking the whole night through and marveled at how he had managed to ever get much done in his lifetime with that kind of attitude. Then again, she had to remind herself, two hundred years was an awful long time to be left to haunt one place, especially for an explorer, and if the blue rose wasn't properly discovered this time, that would be a whole other fifty years for him in tiny Pilmilton Woods. She should cut him some slack.

"Meriwether," she began gently. "I have a plan."

Meriwether eyed her a little suspiciously. "Do you?"

"Oh, yes. And I've met your great-great-great-great-great-grandniece and she thinks it just might work. It does, however, involve an experiment." Goldenrod waited.

After a moment, Meriwether said, "Well . . . you have my attention."

"Here's the thing. Didn't I sorta, by default, send Snotshot on the quest to find the blue rose?"

Meriwether's eyebrows knitted together slightly, but he managed to keep his voice politely steady when he responded with, "Yes, I believe you did."

"So if she is on the quest, doesn't that mean that she'd be able to see you now?"

One of Meriwether's eyebrows unknitted itself and arched up instead. "I suppose it should."

Goldenrod grinned. "Perfect. So the next part of the plan is, what exactly do you know about being a scary kind of ghost?"

Snotshot lay on the cot in her makeshift bedroom, staring at a poster she had drawn on the back of a large and yellowed piece of paper. The picture was of herself playing a red electric guitar while a huge audience lifted cell phones into the air. The back of the guy in the front row might have even been a happy, smiling version of her dad.

It was amazing how a space with crude stone walls, inexpertly decorated and almost claustrophobically small, could make her feel so amazing. Sure, sometimes she missed her large bedroom at home and its ridiculously comfortable bed. Sometimes she even missed her dad's goodnight hugs. But she didn't miss those nights when she could hear him tossing and turning—and sometimes even quietly crying— and she could do nothing about it. Whatever else the caves lacked, they provided a place where she felt in control. And that feeling was priceless.

She hung upside down from the side of her cot and swept aside the brown blanket she had purposely let drape off of the bed so that it brushed the floor. There, bathing the mattress springs above it in a faint blue glow, almost like it was made out of water, was the jar with the blue roses.

Last night, after she had been sure that everyone else was asleep, Snotshot had taken out the jar and placed it on the little table by her bed. She had to admit—only to herself of course—that the flowers had added a nice touch to her bedroom by somehow making it feel even homier. A little part of her would have liked to keep them.

But then she had had a fabulous dream about becoming a rich and famous flower-finder, and this morning she had woken up with the thought that as nice as the jar of flowers looked in her room, a brand-new, humongous television set would look even nicer. The dream had also convinced her

to trust that the girl had been right about the flowers'
importance after all, which also meant that at some point
very soon she was going to have to follow the rest of the
girl's advice.

Take it to a botanist or scientist, she had said. Snotshot would
have to think long and hard about that one. She certainly
couldn't think of any botanists off the top of her head, and as
for scientists . . . well, the only one who came to mind was
her chemistry teacher from last year whom she knew would
at least remember her well. Unfortunately, the reason he
would remember her involved an unassigned, extracurricular
lab experiment that had left the teacher's desk drawers smell-
ing like a mixture of rotten eggs and radishes for the better
part of the year. And Mr. Elliot seemed like the type that
might hold a grudge.

Then again, it would probably be best if Snotshot found
someone who had nothing to do with her old life and,
preferably, nothing to do with her new life either. After all,
she neither wanted to go back to who she had been nor
did she want to share whatever bounty might be coming
her way with the rest of the kids. She might have to go out
of town for a couple of days to find someone who could
help. She wondered if botanists were listed on the Internet.

She was trying to come up with a clever way to ask
Brains for some information on this when, suddenly, a voice
that sounded like a howling wind rustling through dark

trees whispered right into her ear, "You must give it back."

Her head snapped up at once. As the blood rushed to it, her vision whitened, and it took a few seconds for her eyes to focus enough to realize that what lay before them was one of the most terrifying visions she had ever seen.

BRILLIANT TROUBLEMAKERS

Meriwether Lewis had always been a good student, even when alive, of course. He had an uncanny ability to know what bits of things to pay attention to in order to get the most out of the information being given him. This combined with his verve, instinct, and knack for improvisation were all the things that had made him a legendary explorer.

Now, they were helping him to be the scariest ghost he could possibly be. If there was one thing Meriwether liked, it was excelling at whatever it was he set his mind to.

After telling him her plan, Goldenrod had also given him some pointers so that now he stood before the gaping girl with ghostly shackles and chains around his arms and legs that he was rattling relentlessly. He had turned his spiffy maroon coat into a moth-ridden and bedraggled mess (luckily, ghostly fabric was much easier to mend than the real kind, as Meriwether had never been much of a tailor to speak of). He had changed his voice to be a slippery, sinewy, and altogether creepy kind of whisper.

Then, he had taken some liberties of his own. Around his head, he had fashioned a sort of large and fiery wreath. It perfectly matched the two burning flames in his eyes that had taken the place of his blue pupils. His head itself was changing color from red to blue and back again, so that at one moment the wreath looked like burning fire, and the next like sharp daggers of ice. If it should prove necessary, he was prepared to set his head spinning along its neck.

He hadn't had this much fun in years.

The same probably couldn't be said for the girl, who was noticeably shaking as she stared up at him.

"The woods require the roses back. You must leave the jar at the small clearing at the edge of the woods. You must, you must, you must," Meriwether hissed.

The girl continued to look scared, but a glimmer of something appeared in her eyes.

"The roses must be sacrificed to keep the spirits at bay. You cannot keep them. You must return the jar to the clearing at the edge of the woods. You must, you must, you must," Meriwether continued.

"I . . . ," the girl started and then, after taking a deep breath, "and what if I don't?" she said in a rush of words, almost as if she were reading the lines of a kick-butt action star.

The glimmer of something Meriwether had seen in her was defiance, and certainly more than a little bravery. Despite his mission, whose sole purpose was to scare the living daylights out of her, the ghost was impressed. After all, those were two qualities that were near and dear to the heart of any explorer worth his weight in fantastic discoveries.

"Then," Meriwether boomed, suddenly turning up the volume on his whisper so that his voice clattered against the cavern walls like a flock of jet-black ravens into a midnight sky, "I shall haunt you for the rest of your life!"

Despite his admiration, Meriwether Lewis was not someone to botch a mission.

The girl flinched and eyed the jar underneath the bed, although she did not move.

Meriwether started to chant, "The woods require the roses. You must give them back. You must. You must. You must." He was able to multiply his roaring voice so that it now sounded like a chorus echoing from every corner of the stone walls. The sound was so loud and so otherworldly, that it almost became visible, like an eerie fog that had filled up the tiny room. This had been an idea of Goldenrod's, who had apparently seen something similar in a horror movie that she'd accidentally, and unbeknownst to her mother, caught on TV one night.

Meriwether had just hooked his thumb on to his right

ear, about to give his head a big push to send it spinning, when the girl finally became unfrozen from her spot.

In a flash, she grabbed the jar from underneath the bed and went flying out of the room.

Meriwether paused a moment, and then, with a satisfied and dignified little nod, disappeared. His work was done.

✳

Brains was rubbing his elbow. Snotshot had hit it quite hard as she had jetted past him out of the cavern. She looked like she had seen a ghost.

He wondered what could have possibly set her off. Maybe going through with the plan was a bad idea. After all, who was really to say that the Morams hadn't told anyone about it?

Yesterday, when he'd discovered the two of them were gone, he had been furious with Lint. As usual, Lint took the abuse with a scowl, but silently. After Brains had calmed down a bit, Lint had eventually pointed out that the two kids would probably be too weak and too scared to ever reveal anything to anyone. To Brains's surprise, Snotshot had, for once, heartily agreed with him.

"I bet if they can find a way to give themselves amnesia, they're doing it," Snotshot had said confidently. "We'll be fine."

A little while later, No-Bone had come back and told them about his run-in with what turned out to be Toe Jam's grandmother, and the look of horror on the Morams' faces when they found out about their mother's garden. "They're probably still crying their eyes out," he said, totally agreeing with the assessment that their plan was foolproof. "I don't think Toe Jam is going to be coming back tonight, though," No-Bone had added.

Lint had waited a moment before saying almost cheerfully to No-Bone, "So you let them escape too!"

"What?" No-Bone had said indignantly. "I certainly did not! I was under attack!"

"By an old lady?" Snotshot had asked with raised eyebrows.

"Believe me, this was no ordinary old lady."

By this morning, the rest of the gang had so boosted Brains's confidence, that he was the one calmly reassuring Spitbubble that they wouldn't need to change their plans despite the Morams' escape. Spitbubble had listened carefully and then quickly agreed with his assessment.

Now, though, Brains was again starting to have his doubts. He furrowed his eyebrows a bit as he looked around the cavern. No one else seemed to have a care in the world. Lint was sitting in a corner fussing about with his belly button. No-Bone was doing some extremely impressive, though painful-looking, stretching exercises against a corner of the wall, and Spitbubble was sitting on a tan leather armchair that he had brought in from god-knows-where sometime last week. He was rummaging through the green backpack that the Morams had left behind, unceremoniously tossing notebooks and papers aside.

So far, everything seemed perfectly normal. Except that Snotshot had just flown out of the cavern like she was being chased by rabid dogs. If nothing else, she was a part of the plan, and they needed her. Suddenly, Brains felt like he'd be remiss if he didn't at least mention something about his worries to Spitbubble.

He walked over to the armchair.

Spitbubble was throwing the final bits of paper out of the green backpack. They seemed to be filled with some interesting-looking diagrams. Brains tilted his head to get a closer look when Spitbubble crumpled up all the papers and stuffed them back into the bag. "Nothing interesting or useful here, except probably to that bratty girl," Spitbubble said calmly. "No-Bone."

No-Bone looked up (or would it be down?) from his headstand.

Spitbubble held the backpack away from him dismissively. "Throw this in the river. If that girl ever comes looking for it, I want to be sure that she never sees it again."

No-Bone flipped onto his feet, grabbed the bag from Spitbubble, and walked out of the cavern.

"Serves her right," Spitbubble said with a sneer. "Thinking she could outmaneuver me."

Brains frowned. That was just the thing; Goldenrod Moram was actually pretty smart. "Spitbubble . . . ," Brains began.

Spitbubble leaned back into his armchair. "I know."

"You do?" Brains said, somewhat relieved. He was starting to feel like maybe he was just being paranoid for no reason, but if Spitbubble was having some doubts too, then they could definitely convince the other kids . . .

"I'm not gonna lie, you do have some reason to ask for this," Spitbubble said. "You sorta . . . deserve it."

Huh? Brains blinked in confusion.

"I know that without that crazy brain of yours, we wouldn't be able to come up with half the stuff we do. And I want you to know that I *am* grateful. And, yes, after this mission we can work on giving you a slightly higher position. A second-in-command sort of deal, officially."

Brains was taken aback. It was the first time Spitbubble had so openly acknowledged his contributions.

"Now, I don't want you getting too full of yourself," Spitbubble said with a smirk.

Brains shrugged. "It ain't bragging if you can back it up, right?" he said quietly.

Spitbubble gave a short, loud snort, which was as close as most of them ever got to hearing him laugh. He rose from the chair and gave Brains a quick pat on the back. "We should get going soon, right?"

Brains nodded. It was stupid to doubt himself. No one else did. They all relied on him, even Spitbubble, so of course he could do this. They had thought about and rehearsed this plan for so long; everything was going to be completely fine. Morams or no Morams.

All he had to do now was find Snotshot.

✳

When Goldenrod saw Meriwether next, he still had the ghostly manacles on his wrists and the wreath of flames around his head, but the fact that he was grinning from ear to ear somewhat ruined the effect.

"It worked?" she asked him.

"Indeed!" Meriwether said and pointed to a spot in the clearing that looked freshly dug up. "I made her bury it in case you were not the first person to come in here after her."

"Good thinking," Goldenrod said.

"I should say the same to you," Meriwether said with a little bow.

Goldenrod grinned. "I have just enough time to get the roses out of here before this afternoon, and then tomorrow . . . What's wrong?" she asked as suddenly she saw Meriwether's expression go from elated to apologetic. He was kicking one of his ghostly chains with his toes.

"Er . . . right. About that," Meriwether said. "The thing is, I may not have told you about the *entire* quest."

"What do you mean?" Goldenrod asked.

"As it so happens, this blue rose is only the twin of another blue rose. And you need the second blue rose to get this one out." Meriwether smiled at Goldenrod hopefully.

Goldenrod was not amused. "What?"

"This blue rose," Meriwether said louder, "is a twin—"

"No, never mind. I heard you the first time. But what are you talking about? What do you mean twin blue roses?"

"Um. Well, I'm afraid I can't tell you that part," Meriwether said sheepishly.

"You can't tell me?"

"It's part of the quest, you see. For you to figure out."

Goldenrod stared at Meriwether. "You're saying, you knew this whole time that I wouldn't be able to take the blue rose out of the forest without this other blue rose."

"Right," Meriwether said.

"But you chose not to tell me?"

"Oh, no, no. I didn't *choose* not to tell you. I *couldn't* tell you. It's part of the quest—"

"Oh, forget the quest," Goldenrod said angrily. "What was the point of this whole thing if I could never even get the rose out of the forest?" She turned on her heel and started to stomp out of the clearing.

"But Goldenrod, it shouldn't be so hard for you, really. You have almost a full week to figure out where the other blue rose is. Goldenrod, come back!" Meriwether called in a panic.

His voice was getting fainter as Goldenrod marched out of the forest, her anger outshining all of her other tangled-up emotions.

29

THE PLAN IN ACTION

It was nearly 4:00 p.m., but the sky was still blazing like it was high noon. No-Bone was sweating again in his leather jacket. Somehow he'd convinced himself it would be good luck to keep it on.

They were in the back lot of the Pilmilton Science Museum, leaning against the gray building. Lint was holding on to the shopping cart he had taken from the small supermarket across the street. They were all being much quieter than any of them had ever been before. No-Bone could tell they were all at least a little nervous. Not him, though. He lived to perform.

The museum was closed on Thursdays, so there was no one in the back parking lot—which was strictly reserved for museum visitors—except for one lone purple sedan parked in a corner. No-Bone assumed it belonged to the security guard on duty.

Still, they all looked around carefully to make sure no one was watching before Brains walked over to the small white box right outside the door and quickly punched in the alarm's security code he'd spied through his telescope a couple of weeks ago. Then, Spitbubble used the janitor's keycard No-Bone had gotten hold of to open the back door itself. Once he did, Spitbubble slipped in, followed by Brains, Snotshot, No-Bone, and finally, Lint and the shopping cart, which he carried so that it wouldn't make any noise. They still hadn't seen Toe Jam all day, but they'd shrugged it off, since he was never supposed to take part in the day's plans anyway.

They made their way quietly through the short hallway that led to the double doors of the museum's first floor. Brains had a stopwatch in his hand. He checked his wristwatch and then, at a particular moment, set the stopwatch to start.

Brains had figured out that the museum's cameras ran on a specific timer. Every ten seconds, five of the cameras would display in the control room where the sole guard was on duty. That meant that every camera had forty seconds where it would be dark. After collecting all of their grids and charts from the entire summer, Brains had figured out where exactly No-Bone would have to be at every second, and No-Bone, of course, had finessed it.

When Brains motioned for him to go, No-Bone didn't just saunter to his first checkpoint. Oh no. He was going to make this a much more exciting experience. He knew that he could do a cartwheel followed by a triple flip in just under nine seconds. So he did.

He briefly caught the rest of the kids staring with their mouths agape and then Snotshot rolling her eyes. He just smirked. If there was one thing the circus clowns had taught him, it was never to blow a perfect opportunity to show off.

Brains opened his mouth to say something, but there was no time for him to say it, because in a moment, No-Bone had to be off again, and in fourteen seconds, he was in an entirely different wing.

The kids couldn't see him anymore, but that didn't stop No-Bone from flipping and somersaulting the rest of the thirty-two seconds it took for him to get to his destination. Because if there was one thing the acrobats had taught him, it was never to pass up an opportunity to practice.

His destination—for the moment—was a pillar by the museum's technology exhibit. No-Bone stretched and positioned himself so that he was as tall and straight as the column itself, invisible from the angle the camera was shooting. He eyed the motion sensor-controlled dance floor that was on a stage just behind the pillar. Right now, that stage was a serene blue.

He checked his digital wristwatch and waited, prechoreographing his moves in his head. In a moment came a very small beep. He immediately ran out to the dance floor. It was time to really go wild.

No-Bone broke it down. He pop-and-locked, did headspins, leg flares, bellymills, and a couple of flying leaps for good measure. The floor started going crazy in time with his movements. First it turned all sorts of bright colors and then, as No-Bone's moves started to get more intense, it began to break out into graphics: popping popcorn kernels, shooting rockets, fireworks.

His watch beeped again and in a flash, he was behind the pillar. Ten seconds later, he was slipping into a height machine that set off a red siren and loudly proclaimed that he was five feet two inches (which, incidentally, was completely wrong. He knew for a fact that he had made it to five feet three a few weeks ago).

Ten seconds after that, he was at a neighboring exhibit, causing a giant metal ladder sculpture to move back and forth in waves and then a sphere filled with blue plasma to spin madly on its axis. He had just taken his hands off of the sphere when he heard the sound of footsteps rushing down the hall.

He had time for one more tiny somersault as he rolled himself quickly onto the landing of the museum's stairs, and then quietly sped up them, leaving the security guard to look for a five-foot-two ghost.

✳

As soon as the security guard had left his station, Brains slipped in. It took him hardly any time at all to pop in the

DVD, and set it up so that the TVs were only playing a recorded version of a perfectly empty science museum on a Thursday afternoon.

Once that was done, the group quickly took the back stairway and entered the second floor, where No-Bone was waiting for them, right by the Energy Quest exhibit.

The exhibit was probably every kid's dream, but it was especially Brains's. It had turbines—giant fans—that you could set spinning by using a regular old vacuum cleaner on a smaller fan attached to it. It had a wave machine that let you create giant waves in a little blue pool. It had a plasma station where you could move a coil of hot pink light around with the aid of a magnet. And hovering above it all was Brains's favorite part: a giant Tesla coil that, during demonstrations, would shoot out huge strands of purple lightning. Brains wished he could've found a way to work stealing the coil into their plan; it would look fantastic in his lab. But it was way too bulky. They were going to have their work cut out for them as it was.

Right away, the kids went to the stations they were assigned. Snotshot was unscrewing giant solar panels from the solar energy exhibit, and putting them in her large back-pack. No-Bone was dismantling the pump that was the centerpiece of the geothermal exhibit, which demonstrated how you could use steam from the earth itself (as in, say, a hot spring) to make heat and electricity. These were the two stations Brains thought were most important, given the group's resources in the forest.

As Lint pushed the shopping cart over to help No-Bone out, he stopped to look at the picture of Nikola Tesla that was hanging underneath his coil.

"Hey," Lint said to Brains. "That's the same guy who's hanging in your lab." He bent down to look at the writing underneath the picture. "'Nikola Tesla spent his life trying to find different sources of energy, often from the earth itself,'" he read slowly and deliberately. "Hey, like you!" Lint looked over at Brains.

Brains couldn't help but give a small smile. Getting directly compared to one of your heroes by a friend was no everyday occurrence.

"It's great that you've chosen to demonstrate your ability to read, Lint," came Spitbubble's low voice. "But has it replaced the brain activity reminding you that you have a job to do?"

Lint shut up and quickly pushed the cart over to No-Bone's station.

Brains thought that was a little rich coming from Spitbubble, considering that he had insisted on taking a few minutes during the time Brains was in the control room to show off his own namesake skill to the rest of the group. The giant soap bubble exhibit had probably never seen such an enormous, unbroken sphere in its existence, but still. There was a time and place for everything.

Spitbubble never came with them on their normal missions, but this one was so big that apparently even he'd felt the need to be there. Not that he did much. Currently, he was leaning on the long rod that led to the Tesla coil and watching the rest of the kids like a hawk, waiting to criticize or bark orders depending on whichever needs arose. Sometimes, Brains didn't like the older boy very much. But then he would remind himself of all he had done for the Gross-Out Gang, of all he still planned to do in giving them a permanent home, and he would shoo those thoughts out of his head.

Brains didn't have time for thoughts outside of science now, anyway. He was examining the wave machine. He hadn't planned on taking it, but maybe it would be possible to somehow use it with the stream that ran by his lab. *And maybe*, he thought as he eyed the giant fans, *it might be possible to harness some wind power too.* After all, they could use all the energy they could generate.

"Lint, when you're done over there, come help me take this apart too," Brains said, as he walked over to the hydropower station and started to figure out how to disassemble the wave machine.

Just as he was about to turn the first screw with his screwdriver, he heard what sounded like a giant, inhuman sneeze.

Everyone froze. A few seconds later, there came another one.

And then another.

"It's the exhibit next door," Brains finally said, and they all sighed a little in relief.

"But why is it going off?" No-Bone asked.

"I don't know," Brains said, eyebrows furrowed.

"Snotshot," Spitbubble said, "go investigate."

Snotshot nodded and started to quietly make her way over to the bacteria exhibit down the hall.

30

AN A-HA AND AH-CHOO MOMENT

The hardest part of Goldenrod and Birch's plan came right at the very beginning, when they had to find a way to get into the museum on the heels of the Gross-Out Gang. Goldenrod took the lead there, using her stealth skills to hide behind the corner of the building. Then, as soon as Lint had passed through the door, she quietly sprinted so that before the door could fully close, she had reached it and put a large piece of duct tape over the lock mechanism. When she closed the door seconds later, it looked shut— but it wasn't locked.

Their next step was to go sit by the front of the museum and wait. According to Toe Jam's instructions, they would be clear to enter once the red lights on the cameras were off. That would mean that Brains had gotten into the control room and started the looped DVD and that no one would see them go into the closed museum.

Less than ten minutes later, Birch said, "They're off. Let's go." He led the way around the building to the back door and the Morams slipped in, with Goldenrod peeling off the duct tape before closing the door again. After all, a good explorer never left any evidence behind when dealing with secret operations.

The museum was peaceful and quiet. Goldenrod had been there before quite a number of times with her family, and it was a little odd to see all of the experiment stations lying still, and all of the lab coats and goggles hung up and in their places. As she passed by the cooking experiment station, she specifically recollected the last time she had been there and how excited her dad had been that there was a new exhibit demonstrating two of his favorite hobbies: science and cooking. If there was only a way the curators could have fit home repair in there, the family might have never seen Mr. Moram again.

Goldenrod knew they had to head to the back double doors to get to the stairs and up to Energy Quest, but she took a little detour first. One, because she knew the Gross-Out Gang had distracted the guard with an exhibit that was close by and she wanted to make sure that he was gone. (After all, it wouldn't be very adventurous if the Morams simply tattled on Spitbubble's crew to the authorities . . . without having a little fun with them first.) And two, because Goldenrod couldn't help but pay a visit to *her* favorite exhibit. As long as she was there and all.

Her exhibit was tucked into a front corner. It was a small but loving tribute to the most famous explorers to ever grace their area—so far, anyway: Mr. Meriwether Lewis and Mr. William Clark. The little section had a moss green carpet, and there were a few dioramas under glass showing plastic versions of some of the animals Lewis and Clark had discovered, including Meriwether's—and Cassandra's and Toe Jam's—woodpecker. There was a station where kids could identify five different types of plants based on their characteristics, and there was a nice portrait of Meriwether, maroon overcoat and all. The sight of the familiar overcoat gave Goldenrod a little pang of remorse at how she had behaved the last time she'd seen the ghost. It hadn't been very scientific or rational of her to storm out on him like that. Once she'd had time to think it through, she'd realized that it really hadn't been his fault that she couldn't complete the quest. She hoped she could go back and apologize once this whole thing was over.

Perhaps she was taking a tiny bit longer than she should, but Goldenrod couldn't leave the exhibit without getting a quick look at her favorite part. It hung on the back wall: a very long, faded map under a heavy glass frame, an original. The map was beautiful, precise, and perfect, and it made her hope even harder that its maker wasn't too disheartened with her.

As she scanned the illustrated parchment dreamily, suddenly she gasped. There, on the bottom right-hand corner of

the map, was a blue rose. A blue compass rose. When Goldenrod looked over the map again, she realized, for the first
time ever, what it truly was. It was a map of her forest. And,
not only that, but faint blue lines seemed to be showing
various routes to get out of it—if only you knew what
you were looking at. Suddenly, Goldenrod understood:
one of those routes was the only way to get the real blue
rose out.

"Goldenrod," Birch whispered, "we have to go." He had
been acting uncharacteristically brave all day, but she saw a
little hint of worry nestled in his forehead.

He was right, of course, but it didn't stop Goldenrod
from looking longingly at the map one last time. Maybe
when all this was over, she could figure out a way to bor-
row it from the museum and use it before the roses wilted.

As Goldenrod and Birch quietly made their way up the
museum stairs, they started to hear the sounds of Spitbubble's crew up to their no-good deeds. It was time for the
Morams to put their own plan into action, which was pretty
simple really. Scare them first. And then, if they didn't
leave, get the guard to find them.

The first part of it was easy. Turning on the sneeze
machine in the bacteria exhibit was just a flick of a switch,
and they had the perfect hiding place—behind a giant cardboard cutout of a human body—to wait.

Goldenrod silently rejoiced when she saw that Snotshot

was the one who had come to see what the noise was. She was the one they wanted for maximum effect.

While Snotshot was puzzling over the sneeze machine, Goldenrod and Birch took the opportunity to slip from behind the cutout and scurry to the next exhibit. It was all about the five senses and right by the farthest wall was a giant red pipe with an opening that was meant to be spoken into. To display how quickly sound could travel, the pipe wound all the way around the room and ended in the bacteria exhibit—right around where Snotshot was standing.

Birch put his mouth to the pipe and, using the voice Goldenrod had taught him, hissed, "You must leave the museum. You must, you must, you must."

Goldenrod was impressed with how scary and ghostlike her tiny little brother sounded. Clearly, Snotshot was too, since she jumped about a mile into the air at the sound of his voice. Her eyes widened, and in a flash she was running back to the Energy Quest exhibit. "Guys, I think we have to get out of here!" she squealed.

"What?" came the sound of Brains's voice.

"We have to leave. Now," Snotshot said, her voice shaking.

"What are you—" Brains started.

But just then, there was a tremendous crackle. And then a scream.

"Lint!" They heard Brains's anguished yell.

THE PATH OF THE BLUE ROSE

The giant purple streak of lightning from the ceiling scared Snotshot almost as much as the sound of that ghost had.

When she came to her senses enough to look away from the small, innocent-looking coil that had caused the lightning, she caught a glimpse of Spitbubble hastily pulling away from the coil's base. He had obviously just been leaning on what appeared to be a small, silver switch.

Spitbubble looked in shock, and even more so as he caught sight of something by the hydropower station. When Snotshot followed his gaze, she got sick to her stomach too.

The unexpected sound of the lightning had scared them all, and it seemed as if Lint had tried to run when he'd heard it. Now, however, he was lying flat on his back on the floor, his face completely pale with agony. It was easy to see why, as Snotshot could clearly make out a small, white piece of bone that was sticking out from his shin. That lint ball he was always carrying was rolling away from him; he must have tripped over it.

Brains was with him in an instant, trying to examine the wound. "It'll be okay, Lint. It'll be okay," he said, a bit too frantically for Snotshot's liking.

Lint just moaned helplessly, and even louder when Brains gently tried to lift his foot.

"Can you fix it?" came Spitbubble's deep voice.

"His leg's broken," Brains said. "We have to get him to a hospital."

"No! No hospital. They'll ask too many questions about us. Can't you make a splint or something?" came Spitbubble's less-than-calm reply. When people like Brains and Spitbubble were panicking, this was cause for worry.

Snotshot looked around frantically to see if there was anything she could do to help. And that's when she saw them—the girl and her brother. "You!" she said. They were looking pale as they watched Lint cry out in pain.

The rest of the kids turned to them too, and Spitbubble opened his mouth to say something. But he was interrupted by the faint sound of a door opening from the other end of the hallway, the door that led to the back stairs.

"The guard. He's coming," Brains muttered almost to

himself. He was rummaging in his backpack, obviously trying to find something that might work as a splint.

"Okay," Spitbubble said firmly, "everybody out. Run."

"What?" Brains said incredulously. "What about Lint? He can't move!"

"Leave him," Spitbubble said calmly.

If it was at all possible, Lint's face became a shade whiter still. He looked up at Brains fearfully.

"Are you kidding? No way!" Brains said. He and Spitbubble stared at each other across the exhibit, the tension as taut as the wires in that big coil that had caused this whole mess.

"I can help," Goldenrod spoke up. The entire Gang stared at her again, but it was Snotshot she was looking at. "The rose," Goldenrod said to her. "We can go get it. Can you help me?"

Before Snotshot could even process what the girl was asking, there was the sound of a door opening and closing. Spitbubble was gone. The rest of the Gross-Out Gang looked at one another in shock.

"If she can help, help her," Brains finally said to Snotshot as the sound of the guard's footsteps got closer.

Snotshot took one more look at Lint's agonized expression. "Let's go," she said to Goldenrod. The two of them and Birch quickly walked through the same front door from which Spitbubble had made his escape.

Just as they were running down the stairs, they heard the incredulous sounds of the security guard as he came upon what must have been a very unusual scene for a Thursday afternoon at the museum.

❋

Goldenrod led the way to the Lewis and Clark exhibit as they burst through the first floor's double doors.

"There's a map," she explained to Snotshot. "We have to, um, take it from the museum." The thought made her a little nauseous. But this was an emergency and she hoped that Meriwether—and the museum guard, the police, and her parents—would understand.

"Fine, show me," Snotshot said, and a few seconds later, Goldenrod was pointing at the wall with the beautiful and faded parchment.

The frame was too big for one non-Lint-sized person to carry and run with at the same time. Goldenrod knew she couldn't have done it with just Birch's help either. And since Snotshot already knew what and where the rose and clearing were, it had just made sense to ask her.

And she'd been right. Without a moment's hesitation, Snotshot had taken the frame down from the wall. *She at least has some practice taking things that don't belong to her,* Goldenrod thought.

She and Birch went to help. It was awkward carrying

the long frame among the three of them, especially since there was a pretty profound height difference between Birch and Snotshot. But they stuck Birch in the middle and ran as fast as they could, Goldenrod leading the way. They took the back door out of the museum and ran down through the wooded area that would eventually lead to Pilmilton Woods.

They didn't say much to one another as they ran. Once, Goldenrod mentioned to Birch that they were heading into the forest again. He just nodded in response. The rest of the way, they focused on their speed.

As they were nearing the forest's perimeter, Snotshot called out, "Do you know where the rose is?"

"Yes," said Goldenrod.

"So . . . the ghost. Do you know about him?" Snotshot asked.

Goldenrod hesitated. "Yes," she finally said and then looked back at Birch. His face looked grim, but he didn't make any remarks about this new development.

"Do you think he'll turn up?" Snotshot asked, sounding a little frightened at the prospect.

"No," Goldenrod said. "I don't think you should worry about him." This probably wasn't the best time to confess that Meriwether would never have turned into Snotshot's worst nightmare without Goldenrod's help.

In a few minutes, they had reached the forest and, soon after, the clearing. Goldenrod gently put down her section of the map and went over to the spot where the jar was buried. She kneeled down and started to dig with her hands. Within a few moments, she had taken out the glowing jar. The blue roses were still inside it, though looking dimmer than when she had seen them on the bush.

"Now what?" Snotshot asked.

"The map," Goldenrod said as she walked over to them with the jar. "It will show us the only possible route to get the rose out of the forest. See?" She knelt down in front of the map, where the blue compass rose was now glowing faintly too, probably because it was so near its other half. Only one of the many blue paths Goldenrod had noticed before was visible now, and it was also shining.

"Let's go, then," Snotshot said.

"We have to take the map back too. It's priceless," Goldenrod said.

Snotshot opened her mouth to speak, when they heard a booming voice instead.

"Priceless? You don't say. I think that means it should stay right here, then."

They whipped around to see Spitbubble walking swiftly toward them.

"Oh no," groaned Birch.

And then, the most extraordinary thing happened. Snotshot turned to the Morams and said, "You run back with the rose. Help Lint. I'll take care of this."

"But the map—" Goldenrod started.

"Can you memorize the path?" Snotshot asked.

"Yes—" Goldenrod said. "But we can't let him take it."

Snotshot looked down at the frame at her feet. "Yeah," she said. "I know. Look, I'll make sure the museum gets it back. You have my word." She brought her head up and looked Goldenrod square in the eye.

Slowly, Goldenrod nodded. "Okay," she said. "I trust you."

"Go help Lint," Snotshot said simply.

Goldenrod nodded again and then, jar in hand, she and Birch started to run as fast as they could out of the forest.

❁

"Hey, where do they think they're going?" Spitbubble glared at the vanishing figures of Goldenrod and Birch.

Snotshot turned around to face him. "To help Lint. He's hurt, Spitbubble. But you already knew that."

Spitbubble snorted. "Please. Why would they help him? How *could* they even help him? They're just two dumb brats. I think you got played." He pointed to the frame. "Hand that over."

"What?"

"You know what. That *priceless* map."

Snotshot hesitated for only a moment. Then she said, "No."

"What do you mean, no?" Spitbubble asked in his lowest, most menacing voice.

"The map is going back to the museum. I gave Goldenrod my word," Snotshot said.

Spitbubble let out a short laugh. "Oh, really? How do you propose to get it out of here exactly? Are you going to take me on, one on one?"

Inwardly, Snotshot shuddered a little. She had never been in a fight with Spitbubble, and he was older and bigger than she was. The chances of her actually getting the map out of there were slim to say the least. Outwardly, however, she couldn't let him see that. Luckily, she *was* a pretty good actress.

"If that's what it takes," she responded coolly.

"Seriously?" Spitbubble asked.

"Yeah, seriously," she said.

"You really want to do this?"

"If I have to." Snotshot was beginning to suspect that maybe Spitbubble was stalling because he hadn't been in as many fights as he let on either.

He sighed. "All right. It's not usually my policy to hit a girl, but if you're asking for it." He looked greedily at the map, but he didn't make a move.

Suddenly, a streak of courage exploded within Snotshot. It might have had something to do with being called a girl. "I can't believe you!" she yelled. "I can't believe you left us there. What good is a rigged-up cavern if all of us end up in jail? What were you going to do, just hang out there by yourself?"

Snotshot expected Spitbubble to give some excuse, any excuse. Instead, he was silent.

"Wait . . . ," Snotshot said, her mind reeling. "Is that true? Were you not going to let us stay there?"

"Of course I was," Spitbubble said. "I've done everything for you guys. Everything."

The problem was that Spitbubble wasn't nearly as good an actor as Snotshot was.

"From where I stand," Snotshot said slowly, "it looks like we've been doing everything for you." She turned around and started to walk away.

"Just where do you think you're going?" Spitbubble asked.

"Back to the museum. I'm returning the map, and I'm going to face whatever it is my friends are facing."

"Your *friends*?" Spitbubble sneered.

Snotshot whipped back around. "Yes, my friends," she said hotly. "And it's a lot more than you have."

"What," Spitbubble started, "are you talking about? They *are* mine. I own them. I own all of you."

"You don't own me. Not anymore." Snotshot found that she wasn't even acting as she lifted the map over her head and started to make her way back out of the forest.

The frame was heavy, and she couldn't move very fast with it.

But, somehow, she wasn't that surprised when she didn't hear the sound of footsteps behind her.

THE COOKIE STRATEGY

By the time Goldenrod and Birch had gotten back to the science museum, there was a cop car and ambulance there, and a small crowd had gathered to gape at the large kid on a stretcher and two other kids being questioned by a police officer. All three looked miserable, and Goldenrod couldn't help but notice that Brains was casting worried glances toward Lint in between answering the cop's questions.

Goldenrod and Birch had made their way to the front of the crowd and asked the paramedic wrapping up Lint's leg if they could talk to him for a second.

"He's our friend," Goldenrod said, and the paramedic looked at her worried face and nodded.

"All right," she said. "Just for a minute. Then we've got to get him to the hospital. His leg is broken in three places."

Lint grabbed on to the paramedic's arm. "But I can run

the annual Cookman half marathon, right? It's not for another three weeks."

The paramedic raised her eyebrows. "Honey, you're not going to be running anywhere for a long time. It's going to take you at least a few months just to walk."

Lint groaned as the paramedic went to talk to her partner who was driving the ambulance. "My dad will *never* notice me now," he said miserably, his face still pale and clammy-looking from pain.

Goldenrod tried to give a reassuring smile to her former Formidable Foe. "It's okay, Lint," she said gently. "I can help."

Lint furrowed his brow a tiny bit but didn't say anything.

Goldenrod looked around to make sure no one was watching her. Luckily, they all seemed much more interested in the interrogation taking place than in the patient visit happening on the side. She did catch Brains's eye, but him she wasn't worried about so much. She took the jar with the blue roses out from her backpack, quickly unscrewed it, and delicately touched a petal to the exposed skin on Lint's ankle. His skin glowed for a moment, and she could tell from the jolted look that appeared on his face that suddenly his pain was gone. He looked down. His leg was all bandaged up, but Goldenrod had a feeling that the paramedic was going to have a bit of a surprise when she unwrapped it.

She and Birch quickly and quietly slipped away before Lint, or anyone else, had a chance to say anything.

✳

As Goldenrod kneaded a particularly stubborn piece of dough, she smiled to herself, thinking about the jar of blue roses that was now safely tucked away in one of her desk drawers.

She had plans to show the flowers to her father, the scientist, and her mother, the gardener, very soon, of course. After all, they wouldn't keep in that jar for much longer, and they absolutely needed to get properly discovered. But there was just one more thing she and Birch needed to do before they could get to that.

It was the weekend and, since their dad was home, Goldenrod and Birch had convinced him to spend it baking batches upon batches of cookies.

Baking with Mr. Moram was always fun, as he seemed to consider the art more of a chemistry experiment than a culinary one. He loved testing out all sorts of new flavor combinations, or rising agents, or simply a new way to sweeten a sweet. Whenever he baked, he would pour the entire contents of the pantry out onto the countertop to assess the ingredient situation. Then he would line up measuring cups, beakers, pots, pans, and utensils like an army battalion on the opposite countertop. After a brief "pep talk"—this is what

Goldenrod chose to call her father's process of walking round and round the kitchen muttering to himself—he would begin the attack: chopping, mixing, kneading, beating, slicing, dicing, toasting, roasting, and sometimes flambéing on his way to possible pastry nirvana.

Goldenrod and Birch loved every minute of it. But, on this day, although they were glad as always to be a part of their father's kooky chemical warfare, they realized part of the reason they were baking was a rather sad one.

Their mother had been inconsolable for a whole day now—ever since she had woken up to discover that the entire garden and lawn was a wasteland of wilted plants. The grass hadn't just dried up; it had basically disintegrated so that all that were left were small patches of cropped, dark brown stalks. The chrysanthemums, hydrangeas, dahlias, and tulips were just blackened silhouettes of themselves. Only a few lone goldenrod stalks had survived Brains's very effective attack, looking like a couple of sad flowers stuck on a badly balding head.

Cookies were just one item in a long list of ideas the rest of the Morams had cooked up in order to try and make Mrs. Moram feel better (various crayon drawings, "#1 Mom" mugs, and even a plastic dancing flower that moved when you whistled Pachelbel's Canon quite precisely had all preceded it).

But Mr. Moram looked hopeful as he peered at his kids

through his safety goggles. "This could be it, kiddos. This could be the cheering potion your mom needs." He took a big bite out of a nutmeg-basil–jelly roll, and screwed up his face as he chewed slowly and thoughtfully. "Hmmm," he finally said. "I'm not sure the basil is cooperating here. Perhaps it's time to call in the parsley!" And with that he had dashed off to round up the leafy green and attempt a new blend.

But even if Mom doesn't like that one, Goldenrod thought, *there are so many others to choose from: strawberry-cranberry-lemon snaps; peanut-butter–popcorn clusters; choco-vanilla–oyster-cracker crumbles.* And with every batch, Goldenrod made sure to take the most appetizing, scrumptious-looking ones and set them aside in a large brown cardboard box that she and Birch had hidden in one of the lower cabinets.

By midafternoon, the Morams were out of supplies, and all they had managed was a very weak smile out of Mrs. Moram as she had bitten into an oatmeal-carrot-cinnamon concoction. Goldenrod and Birch still felt pretty awful, but it gave them more of a boost to put the second part of their baking plan into action.

Around 3:00 p.m., they told their mom they were going to go bike riding, promising to stay close. They took the big brown box full of cookies with them.

Goldenrod strapped it down straight to the handlebars of her bike, first wrapping the box in tissue paper and then using a large wad of duct tape. It was extremely important that the box and cookies looked as pristine and delectable as possible.

Then they set off with Goldenrod leading the way. They rode slowly so as not to disturb the cookies. It took them almost half an hour to reach the block they wanted.

As soon as they turned the corner, Goldenrod stopped her bike.

"Okay, Birch. This is my stop. You sure you're cool with doing this?"

Birch nodded. "I'm ready." He hopped off his bike and started to help unduct-tape the package from Goldenrod's handlebars. The tissue paper left the box looking perfect.

"And if he answers the door?" Goldenrod asked.

"Well . . . then I guess he's just gonna have to face me again," Birch said.

Goldenrod laughed. "All right, I'm going to hang back here. She can't see me. But I can see you from here. And you know the signal if you need help."

Birch nodded. "Run and scream."

He slowly started to walk his bike past the houses, toward the gray one with the black roof. He checked the house number against the one they had carefully copied on to the box from the Internet. Then he turned into the driveway and put on his most official-looking, most beaming smile. He didn't turn back to look at Goldenrod, but she was watching him.

With one deep breath, he rang the doorbell. Goldenrod

started to silently pray . . . but before she could get too far along, her prayers had already come true. *She* had answered the door.

"Are you Ms. Barbroff?" Birch asked brightly.

Ms. Barf looked at the tiny, moptopped person standing before her. She sniffed suspiciously. "Yes . . . ," she finally said.

"I have a delivery for you!" Birch held the large brown box in front of him. It was tied up with a nice blue ribbon and seemed to have the name of a fancy bakery printed on it.

Ms. Barf didn't reach out for it. "Who's it from?"

"I'm not sure, ma'am. There's usually a card inside. We offer that as a free service to our customers." Birch beamed.

"You work for this . . . company?" Ms. Barf pointed toward the sign on the box.

"Yes, ma'am," Birch said.

"Humph," Ms. Barf retorted.

Birch offered the box up again.

Come on, take it! Goldenrod silently commanded her ex-teacher.

Finally, Ms. Barf did. "Fine. I'll take it." She looked at Birch sharply as if daring him to ask her for a tip.

But Birch simply grinned radiantly and got back on his bike. "Have a great day, Ms. Barbroff."

She frowned at him as he sped off, and both he and

Goldenrod could hear her saying, "Humph. Looks a little too young to be working if you ask me. His parents better be careful all this early independence doesn't turn him into a hoodlum."

Only after she had slammed the door behind her did Goldenrod and Birch stop at a bush on the corner, trying to get over a fit of giggles.

SWEET REVENGE

Spitbubble lay on his bed in his darkened room. He had purposefully shut off the lights and drawn all the blinds tightly so that he could think.

Things had gone horribly wrong somehow. And he was not a person who was used to things going wrong. Since the museum debacle two days ago, he had found himself craving the dark more and more, thinking that if he could just block out the light, he could make order out of everything—like Brains could. Some of the things Snotshot had said had left him with an odd twinge at having left the four of them at the science museum to fend for themselves: it was wormy and unpleasant, and he didn't much like to dwell on it. It made him feel almost . . . uncool.

There had to be a way to regain control and come out stronger.

"Stannie," he heard his mother call from downstairs.

He didn't stir, instead shutting his eyes to further block out the nagging voice.

"Stannie, come down here, sweetheart. I've got something that will cheer you up."

Spitbubble very much doubted that was true. For one thing, there was no way his mother knew the kinds of things that actually could cheer him up—delicious things like torments and threats and, perhaps sweetest of all, revenge.

"Stannie," his mother's voice called. "Come downstairs!"

He sighed loudly. How could a person be expected to plot dastardly deeds with all that noise?

Heavily, he got himself out of bed and left his bedroom, making sure to slam the door and thunder down the stairs.

"What?" Spitbubble said with a huff as he came into the kitchen.

His mother was standing at the counter, a large cardboard box open in front of her. Inside the box were rows and rows of cookies. It looked like there were at least a dozen kinds, and some of them seemed very weird. One was an odd shade of green, and he could see something resembling a lima bean sticking out of another.

Spitbubble shook his head. Of course she would think that stupid gourmet cookies would be the answer to his problems. Unlike his mother, Spitbubble had never understood the whole fascination with hoity-toity foods, things like caviar (fish eggs) and pâté (duck liver), which were clearly quite disgusting, but which someone had decided must taste delicious simply because they were expensive. But he also knew his mother was a woman who liked to pretend that she was fancy.

Ms. Barbroff was hovering one bony hand over the box, trying to choose the first cookie to try. She must have been feeling particularly adventurous to go for one of the green ones.

Then she offered the box to him. "Look what someone sent me," she said. "Have one." She took a big bite out of her cookie.

"Who sent it to you?" Spitbubble growled, eyebrows furrowed.

"Hmmm," Ms. Barbroff said as she chewed . . . and chewed . . . and chewed. "Maybe it's an acquired taste." She frowned at the cookie, bits of which seemed to be stuck to her teeth.

"Who sent them to you?" Spitbubble asked again.

"Oh, wait. I think there's a note." Ms. Barbroff had spotted a piece of paper underneath the empty space her cookie had left in the box. She grabbed the end of it and carefully pulled it out. It was fancy, heavy beige paper.

"'Dear Ms. Barbroff,'" she read, trying to enunciate the letters around the bits of stuck cookie in her mouth. "'I hope this gift finds you well.'

"'Your son is a thief, a kidnapper, and a general bad guy. For the past few months, he has been leading a group of young, for lack of a better word, hoodlums.'"

It was a bit of a shocker to hear this coming out of a cookie box. Spitbubble immediately lifted the cover and looked at the fancy label on it for the first time. BIRCH'S BATCHES, it said in scrawling cursive, A DIVISION OF G-ROD™ BAKERIES. It was overlaid upon a stunning picture of a bouquet of yellow flowers fanning over a white tree trunk. There was a golden embossed seal closing the box that had the words LEGENDARY ADVENTURERS stamped on it.

With horror, Spitbubble looked at the cookies. "What the . . . ," he started.

But his mother read on. "'They have been doing horrible things all over town. You might have read about some of his followers in the paper yesterday in relation to a particular science museum.'"

"Is this a joke?" Spitbubble yelled, something his low and level voice was not used to doing. With a swing of his hand, he knocked the entire box of cookies to the floor.

But Ms. Barbroff did not pay much attention to the mess. "'If you don't believe me, I have drawn a map that approximately shows where their hideout is. (It would be more accurate, except your son caused me to lose a lot of my possessions in the forest a few days ago.)'" Ms. Barbroff stared at the map that adorned the bottom of the note. PILMILTON

WOODS it said in block letters, and there were pictures of trees and bushes with annotations like SUGAR MAPLE TREES. In the center of all the foliage was a detailed drawing of a very odd structure labeled STAN'S EVIL LAIR.

"This is . . . this is . . . ," Stan sputtered, realizing he was losing control of the situation.

"'If you still don't believe me'"—Ms. Barbroff seemed almost in a trance now as she continued reading the letter—"'I have also included the phone number of a Mrs. Cassandra Lewis of the famous Lewis family. She can give you a very detailed list of items Stan has stolen.'

"'Hope you enjoy the rest of your summer! Dutifully, Goldenrod Moram. P.S. The cookies are not poisoned.'"

Slowly, Ms. Barbroff looked at her son, who was surrounded by scattered cookies and looked as if his legs were stuck to the ground with the same paste that was finally starting to disintegrate in her mouth. "Goldenrod Moram," she said quietly. "But how . . . how does *she* know you?"

Spitbubble straightened up and cleared his throat. It was time to play to his strengths. "I think . . . I think I might have run into her in town somewhere," he started, concentrating at first on controlling his voice again.

"She was one of my students . . ."

"Yes, she seemed like she would have been a difficult one." He hesitated only slightly.

"Yes . . . ," Ms. Barbroff started.

"Rather nasty to me actually . . . Was she nasty to you?" He was much more confident now.

"She gave me a lot of grief," Ms. Barbroff said shakily, and he could see her eyeing yesterday's newspaper, which was still sitting on the kitchen table.

"That must be it, then. She must know I'm your son. That would explain her attitude." His voice was back to normal, he was thankful to notice, and he was back to being in charge.

Ms. Barbroff looked down at the note. He could almost see the sedating voice in her head saying to her, "Yes, that must be it."

"Don't be upset, Ma. Why don't you go relax on the couch? I'll clean this up." It was a nice touch, if Spitbubble did say so himself. And once his mom was out of the room, he would figure out exactly what to do about that girl.

Ms. Barbroff nodded, back to normal again. "Yes, all right," she said slowly and walked to the kitchen door.

But then, as she passed the wall phone on the way out, she suddenly grabbed the receiver. "I'll just make one phone call," she said as she looked down at the beige piece of paper.

For once in his life, Spitbubble was speechless.

34

THE GOLDENROD AND BIRCH EXPEDITION

The day Goldenrod found herself in the forest clearing again was another beautiful and sunny summer day. Amid the chirping birds and buzzing insects, her voice rang out, calling Meriwether's name.

A part of her was afraid that she was too late. She very much wanted to see the ghost again, but she had decided to wait until she was sure the quest was complete so that she could bring him the good news herself. She had then realized, of course, that she didn't quite know how this part would work. At what point exactly did Meriwether's spirit get set free? And what did that even really mean?

"Meriwether," she called out again, crossing her fingers behind her back in the hopes that he would answer.

The fifth time that she said his name, he did.

With a pop, the tall, elegant ghost appeared, beaming at

Goldenrod, though he was most certainly much fainter than ever before.

"You're still here. I'm so glad!" Goldenrod said.

"You completed the quest," Meriwether said.

"Yes, I gave a rose to my dad who took it to the head of his department, and my mom took one to her gardening club. And I had Charla check them against her *Encyclopedia of North American Flora and Fauna*. Your lost discovery has officially been discovered. I even brought the letter from the Horticultural Society." Goldenrod unzipped her backpack and took out a much folded, unfolded, and refolded piece of stationery. "You were right, of course. They said it's looking likely that this is one of the most important natural discoveries of the past fifty years."

"More like the past two hundred years, I'd say," Meriwether said with a smile as he nodded at Goldenrod's letter. "Will they be crediting you with the discovery?"

"Well, yes . . . ," Goldenrod said.

"Good," Meriwether replied.

"Meriwether," Goldenrod started sheepishly, "I also wanted to say I'm sorry for getting mad about the twin roses."

"Oh, no need. No need," Meriwether said cheerfully. "I'd be lying if I said there wasn't a time or two Billy Clark and I had a little tiff, eh?"

Goldenrod smiled. "But, anyway. I am sorry."

Meriwether tilted his head, his transparent eyes beaming. "I think I always had an inkling that you would be the one to finally beat the obstacles. Well done, Goldenrod."

"Obstacles? You mean Spitbubble?"

Meriwether nodded.

"But . . . he hasn't been here for two hundred years, has he?" Goldenrod asked with widened eyes.

Meriwether chuckled. "Oh no. Of course not. He and his band are just a bunch of regular kids . . . well, a bit more diabolical than most, perhaps. But anyone sent on the quest would have had their own set of obstacles to overcome. You have been the only one to fully succeed, obviously."

As Meriwether talked, Goldenrod noticed that he was growing fainter still. His maroon overcoat seemed a creamy pink color now, and there were parts of it that almost blended into the sunlight completely.

Goldenrod frowned slightly. "So what happens to you now?"

"I'm free to go."

"Go where?"

"On," Meriwether said simply.

"But will you be . . ."

"Don't worry about me, Goldenrod," Meriwether said gently. "I'm an explorer. On to new places and new adventures. And so are you, my girl. So are you." The ghost gave her one more fond look and then was suddenly tree and twine and dappled sunlight. He was gone.

Goldenrod stared at the place where he had been. She would probably never see him again, she thought sadly.

Then again, if she had learned anything this summer, it was to never concede to the impossibility of anything and that things like limping ghosts, fantastic flowers, groups of children hiding out in the forest, and fascinatingly odd old ladies were all out there, just waiting to be discovered.

As she turned around to leave the clearing, her heart swelled at that thought and then again when she remembered Meriwether's last words: that she was every bit an explorer too.

✳

Birch held the measuring tape against one oak tree while Toe Jam took the other end and pulled it to another oak.

"Four feet two and a half inches," Toe Jam read off as Birch jotted the number down in his almost-full notebook. Toe Jam let go of the tape, and it went zooming back to Birch's hand.

When Birch looked up, he saw Goldenrod making her way over to them. She had been gone for the past twenty minutes, claiming that she needed to use the bathroom in the old lady's cottage. However, that was most definitely not the direction she was coming from now.

Birch frowned. If there was something else going on in this forest that wasn't what it seemed, he would very much like to know about it in advance this time.

"Where were you?" he asked Goldenrod.

"Oh, I took a detour. For a second, I thought maybe we had forgotten a part in that little clearing back there." She pointed behind her.

Birch flipped through the notebook quickly. "We definitely haven't," he said after he had made sure.

When he looked back up at Goldenrod, she was smiling at him. "Yeah, you're right. You know, you do make a really good Clark."

Toe Jam's head snapped up. "You mean William Clark?"

"The very same," Goldenrod said.

"He was an explorer. I'm related to his partner, you know," Toe Jam explained, rather needlessly, to Birch. By this point, Birch had gotten the whole story of what Toe Jam's family crest meant, how Goldenrod had been inspired to take on this whole mapping business in the first place, and even the slightly creepy notion that a ghost had been haunting this very forest. "Meriwether Lewis was my great-great-great-great-great-great-great-great-uncle," Toe Jam continued. Birch had observed that for all his love of everything disorderly and dirty, Toe Jam still had a touch of his parents' pomposity in him.

Goldenrod rolled her eyes a little as she walked over to check Birch's notebook.

"I think we're done here," Birch said.

Goldenrod nodded. "I can hardly believe we've mapped

this entire forest and documented every single plant or creature we've come across," she said proudly, "and all in two
weeks! This would have taken me at least a month alone. I
definitely couldn't have done it without you, Clark."

Birch beamed.

Goldenrod then turned to Toe Jam. "Or you, Sacagawea.
Really, you definitely helped out by knowing the forest so
well. I'm glad your grandma lifted the ban."

Toe Jam shrugged, but Birch thought he could see a
smile as he looked at the ground.

"This is even better than what I had before," Goldenrod said. Birch was glad to hear it. Originally, Goldenrod
had considered going back into the forest to try and recover
her green backpack, but then Toe Jam found out from the
others that Spitbubble had destroyed it. Birch hadn't enjoyed
seeing his sister's crestfallen face when she'd gotten that bit
of news.

"So, what's next?" Birch asked.

"Well, we still have the western, eastern, and southern
parts of town to do. I don't think it'll take as long as the
forest, but the map wouldn't be complete without them,"
Goldenrod said.

Birch nodded. "Think we can get it done before summer vacation ends?"

"We have three weeks. It's not a lot of time. But I think
if you and I hustle . . ."

"Hey, what about me?" Toe Jam asked.

Birch looked over at him, surprised. "I thought your grandmother said you only had to help us with the forest."

"Oh . . . yeah. She did," Toe Jam said. "Right. Never mind."

Birch and Goldenrod exchanged a glance.

"I actually don't know if we can get this done in three weeks with just the two of us, though," Goldenrod started slowly. "So, if you'd like to help, Randy . . . well, we'd be more than happy to have you."

"I . . . well, maybe. I mean now that I've started it, it wouldn't really seem right not to help finish."

Goldenrod smiled. "Cool."

Birch smiled too. Sure, Toe Jam could be showy sometimes, but Birch had actually grown used to him, sort of even liked having him around. And secretly, Birch had always really liked picking the sock fuzz from between his toes too.

"And maybe if we discover an animal or something, we can name it after me this time," Toe Jam said as the three of them started packing up their stuff.

Goldenrod shot him a look. "Let's not get carried away, Randy. Okay?"

THE GARDEN

When Goldenrod, Birch, and Randy returned to the Moram house that afternoon, it looked as busy as it had been over the past week. There were parts of the front lawn and garden that still looked like the surface of a scorched planet, but most of it was being restored to green again.

Randy immediately went over to a corner where Brains and Lint were quietly laying down some new squares of grass. Old Sue's husband, who also happened to be the town judge, was a good friend of Mrs. Moram's and had given the restoration of her garden as one of a few options for their community service. Brains had chosen it almost immediately. Goldenrod supposed it meant that he must have some semblance of a conscience somewhere in there. And, obviously, Lint was going to do whatever Brains did.

Goldenrod smiled secretly as she watched Lint bend and

move with ease, his leg as muscular and strong as ever. She wouldn't be surprised if he won his family's annual half marathon this year. After all, he would have plenty of time to practice, given that he wasn't going to be spending much of it stealing protein bars. Come to think of it, Goldenrod hadn't seen his lint ball make an appearance over the past couple of days either. *Perhaps he's lost his taste for them*, she thought amusedly, and then felt a slight jolt of affection for the kid. Just the day before, Lint had returned Goldenrod's yellow baby sock to her. He had even rinsed it out.

"Jonas."

Brains looked up from his work as Goldenrod's dad walked over to him.

"If you're interested, I would very much like it if you were to come into my lab sometime next week. I've heard about some of the, er, work you've been doing. And I could really use your help with this new project. We're trying to find greener sources of energy for Pilmilton, you know," Mr. Moram said.

"Seriously?" Brains asked in surprise.

"Seriously. If what I've heard is true, well, some of the ideas you've had are very impressive. Though, um, not stealing from a museum. You shouldn't do that," Mr. Moram added hastily.

"I would really like that, Mr. Moram," Brains said quietly. "Thank you."

Mr. Moram was whisked away then by order of Mrs. Moram, but when Brains looked up to see that Goldenrod was watching him, he gave her a small smile.

Goldenrod smiled back. Maybe, like her, he also had happy memories of the last time they had been in her mother's garden together.

As Goldenrod watched the three members of Spitbubble's Gross-Out Gang digging, her thoughts flitted for a moment to Snotshot. When she had been brought into the police station for questioning, it had been discovered almost immediately that her father had been frantically searching for her ever since she had run away from home. Within hours, they had been gleefully, and apparently somewhat tearfully, reunited, though Goldenrod could barely imagine liquid leaking from some part of Snotshot's face that wasn't her nose. Knowing that the judge had gently suggested that Snotshot be sentenced to some sort of service in her own town, Goldenrod wondered what she was doing now. *Perhaps wiping the snot off of little kids at a day care center,* Goldenrod thought to herself with a smile. *Wouldn't that be ironic?*

As for No-Bone, he actually *was* working with little kids—choosing to volunteer at a gymnastics school that was a couple of towns over. From something Goldenrod had overheard Brains saying, it seemed like the school had even helped to locate an old friend of his in China, whom he was now happily exchanging letters with.

"Goldenrod, could you help Cassandra with that bush?" her mother said as she tossed a pair of orange gardening gloves at her and woke her from her reverie.

"Sure," she said. As Goldenrod put on the gloves, she couldn't help but smile at her mother's giddy expression. It had a lot to do with her garden being so diligently worked on under her careful supervision, for sure, but Goldenrod knew that there was something else that was keeping her so elated these days. As the much-read piece of stationery from the Horticultural Society stated, the discovered blue rose was going to be named just as Goldenrod had requested: *Rosa janine*, after the very best gardener and lover of flora that she had ever known. After all, her mother had named *her* after a flower, so it only seemed fitting to name a flower after her mother. Besides, she couldn't very well name a new species of flower Goldenrod.

Giving Mrs. Janine Moram this piece of news had finally been the trick to getting her to smile again. And now that it looked like her garden would be even more spectacular than it had been before, she was pretty much in a constant state of euphoria.

"Birch, could you come over and help your dad with pulling up some of this old grass?" Goldenrod heard her mother's cheerful voice as she made her way over to where the old lady was packing some dirt around a small bush.

Cassandra looked up at Goldenrod's approach and smiled. "And how did it go today?"

"Well, Pilmilton Woods has officially been mapped in its entirety," Goldenrod said.

"Bravo," Cassandra said. "Is it ready to show your friend Charla yet?"

"Almost." Goldenrod smiled. "I might as well get the rest of Pilmilton in there too. I think she's gonna love it."

"Good," Cassandra said and then lowered her voice so as not to be overheard by the others. "Did you see him?"

Goldenrod nodded. "I said good-bye," she whispered back. "He's gone now."

"He must have been very proud of you, Goldenrod."

"I hope so," Goldenrod said.

"Meriwether Lewis may have dealt with grizzly bears and blizzards and even getting accidentally shot in the thigh by one of his own men . . . but even he never had to deal with Spitbubble."

Goldenrod laughed. "Well, at least Ms. Barbroff proved that she really, really doesn't like hoodlums after all," she said, shaking her head in awe of the fact that her ex-teacher had turned in her own son to the police for his part in the museum escapade.

"And you have to admire her for her consistency," Cassandra said.

"I do," Goldenrod said as she knelt beside the old lady. Not surprisingly, Spitbubble had most certainly not chosen the judge's option to help the Morams with restoring their garden. Goldenrod couldn't imagine that he would be at the gymnastics school with No-Bone either. In fact, it didn't seem likely that he would be facing the rest of the Gross-Out Gang anytime soon. Toe Jam had told Goldenrod and Birch all about what Snotshot had discovered during her confrontation with Spitbubble—that he wasn't really planning on letting them stay in the forest—and his former crew was none too happy about it. *Can't say I blame Spitbubble for staying away,* Goldenrod thought. *After all, they are a pretty formidable group. I wouldn't want any of them going up against me . . . again.*

"All right." Goldenrod turned her attention back to Cassandra. "So what do you need me to do?"

"Go in here and get your hands dirty." Cassandra paused for a moment as her eyes twinkled. "I think having this blue rosebush here will be a good reminder for you, Goldenrod. Just in case you ever think you have to leave your own backyard in search of adventure again."

Goldenrod laughed as she helped Cassandra pack dirt around the bush.

She knew the old lady knew, just as well as she did, that to truly seek adventure, one will always, always have to leave the backyard.

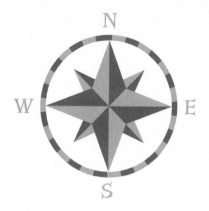

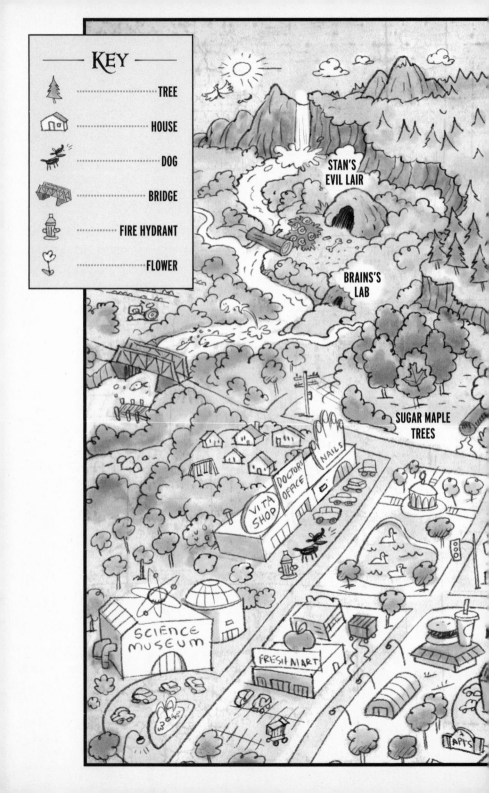

ACKNOWLEDGMENTS

The quest to get this book into your hands has involved the invaluable help and advice of many fellow adventurers who are owed a lot more than my thanks. One is my agent, Marissa Walsh, who took a chance on me and then worked tirelessly to get this book in front of the right person. That person turned out to be Stacy Cantor Abrams, my vastly talented editor at Walker, who saw more in the story than I could ever have seen as a solo explorer and who helped shape it into practically everything that it is.

Speaking of Walker, I think even Lewis and Clark would have been hard-pressed to find a crew that is as dedicated, kind, and talented as the one that has been guiding me through these uncharted territories. A huge thanks to Kim Burns, Katy Hershberger, and Kate Lied—Legendary Adventurers of marketing and publicity. And to Nicole Gastonguay, epic senior designer, for making these pages look so much more magical than I could have even imagined and for the coup that was snagging cover illustrator Gérald Guerlais and "mapmaker" Gideon Kendall.

I owe a lot to those who have traveled alongside me through many more treks than just this one: An enormous amount of gratitude to my amazing friend Katie Spessard, who has read and edited almost everything I've ever written and whose taste, sensibilities, and constructive criticism have made me a far better writer than I could possibly be without her. Being an unpublished writer (or even a published one) means that there are moments when only the most sincere words of encouragement and love can keep you going; for those I am forever grateful to Jenny Goldberg, for being so very good at them, and to Graig Kreindler for being my sense of direction both literally and metaphorically.

A big thanks to two of my favorite writing teachers of all time, Lamar Sanders and Mollie Fermaglich, who not only built my entire foundation of telling a story but also were the first people not obligated by blood or friendship to like my work. To Lisa Hsia, for being a great mentor—and an even better friend—and the kind of boss who takes the whole I'm-quitting-because-I-want-to-work-on-my-novel thing with a very straight face and a lot of words of encouragement.

Goldenrod's quest began in two different writing workshops, so I must thank all those who helped set her on her way from the very start: Carolyn MacCullough, Theresa Drescher, Sharon Garbe, Gabriela Pereira, Nell Mermin, Jenny Ziomek, Kim Kowalski, Mary Fried, Tara Devineni, Bridget Curley, Kelly Sullivan, Julia Kim, Rhonda Atkins, Jennifer Stark, Sarah O'Holla, Andie Levinger, Laura Quinlan Hug, Irene Borland, Kathleen Admirand-Dimmler, Josh Farrar, and Irwin Walkenfeld. Thank you to the Apocalypsies and the Class of 2K12, two groups of fantastic debut authors who have made this past year so much fun as well as far less lonely.

And, of course, my journey would never have started at all without my family. I owe many, many thanks to my parents, Haleh and Hossein, who always made me feel like having a writer in the family was something to be proud of. To my sister, Golnaz, for sharing my sense of humor (and oftentimes her wardrobe). And, finally, to the one person who believed in me beyond anyone else. To my aunt, Homa, who is forever my compass and without whom I can't imagine having made it through this quest or any other.

Corinne Ray

SARVENAZ TASH was born in Tehran, Iran, and grew up on Long Island, New York. She received her BFA in film and television from New York University's Tisch School of the Arts. She has dabbled in all sorts of writing, including screenwriting, copyright, and professional tweeting. *The Mapmaker and the Ghost* is her first novel. Sarvenaz currently lives in Brooklyn, New York.

www.sarvenaztash.com